A GHOST AT HORSE CREEK

by JERI MASSI

LLAMA BOOKS™

Easley, South Carolina 29640

©1989 by Llama Books
821 Lenhardt Road
Easley, SC 29640

Cover design by Dana Thompson
Cover illustration by Del Thompson

Veterinary consultation by William C. Aaroe, D.V.M.

ISBN 1-877778-01-X

1 - Horse Creek Valley

As I drove through the intersection above Horse Creek Valley, I was struck with just how unlikely it was to be in love with a llama rancher. A girl llama rancher, of course.

I had the car windows rolled down to let in the clean spring breeze. Sunlight danced on the dusty hood of my old '79 Pontiac. The air was thick with a jumbled noise of distant tractors, chainsaws, and pickup trucks.

Horse Creek Valley remains unknown to Misters Rand and McNally. Casual readers of road maps would never find it marked out for them, and only the better types of maps would include the name of Horse Creek itself.

Local radio stations (none of which transmit from Horse Creek Valley) lump the whole area together with the Central Savannah River Area, or CSRA. But nobody in the valley really knows that. To them, CSRA refers to "them other folks around Horse Creek Valley."

As my store manager once told me, Horse Creek Valley is the last great bastion of redneckism in America. I had heard other comments even less kind.

To be fair, I would have to admit that several of the farmers in the valley were as modern as any vet could ask. But there were others. The backwards, slow-to-educate-themselves farmers did not seem to believe much in veterinary assistance. And the modern, progressive farmers relied on vets from Augusta to drive out and help them.

I was, after all, young. Most of the men who practiced in the CSRA had been doing so since before I was born. Youth, inexperience, and unemployment had prompted me to accept a position as assistant manager of Belvedere Feed and Seed. Jack Phelps, the owner and manager, had thought it good to have a vet in his employ, and it had seemed to me a likely way to build up a clientele for myself. Enough free assistance might actually convince people to pay for more assistance.

"Don't kid yourself," Jack said. "Folks around here won't pay for anything they used to get for free."

Jack was a hard-bitten sort, without a trace of optimism. He was certainly generous, and an excellent man to work for, but he kept all that a pretty close secret. It had taken me a couple of months to figure out that Jack had a soft heart.

His crustiness was sincere. He expected misfortune out of life, put faith in no man, and always prepared for the worst. He was not sentimental, nor even very gracious. Yet in his ungracious, hard-bitten way, he contributed to half the charities in town and spent every other Saturday visiting senior citizens to do free repair work on their houses for them. He had hired me when I'd needed a job, and he paid me well.

Jack was rather like a character out of my favorite novel series: *No Creature Too Great or Too Small*, written by Wagner Nesbitt, a vet in Scotland who'd practiced about fifty years ago. He had worked with Gilbert Tarnish and Gilbert's brother Sullivan.

Nesbitt's books were full of whimsical and poignant characters, each one full of contradictions, just like Jack, with not a normal one among them. I had read Nesbitt's books while in school, and I think that they, more than anything else, had made me want to specialize in farm work and choose a simple, rural practice. Other classmates of mine, also influenced by *No Creature Too Great or*

Too Small, had chosen the far-flung Rocky Mountains or even the Canadian Yukon. But I had picked the people of Horse Creek Valley, maybe because there was not a normal one among them, either.

Though I had met many characters in Horse Creek Valley, none as of yet had struck me as especially whimsical, and certainly not poignant. But there was Anne.

She was only twenty-one, and we had chatted briefly two or three times. Yet there was something about her that had gone like an arrow into my heart. I even know what it was.

Anne's mother was dead, and Anne ran the farmhouse that sheltered her father and three brothers. They were all big, hardy, and rough-handed men. And yet whenever Anne's father spoke to her or came into her sight, her first response, without fail, was to smile at him.

I had seen him bawl out her brother Billy Bob and even give him a lick or two with a calf rope. But he never raised his voice to Anne.

I supposed, from little things that Anne and her father had said, that when her mother had died, Anne had somehow become a source of cheerfulness and strength that her father had not expected in a daughter. She had entered into his grief with him, and he was grateful to her.

But it was her smile, reserved for him, that had made me fall in love with her so quickly. Anne Hardy knew how to love people. She could draw them right in and make them welcome in her private world.

I already knew that I wanted her to love me and to draw me in, too.

2 - The Llamas

On Anne's twentieth birthday, her father had given her a pasture on the farm to use for any project she chose. Anne chose llamas.

The llamas Anne had named, she had named after storybook characters from Hans Christian Andersen. That one action demonstrated—better than a page of explanation—the love that she had for things beautiful and good and adventurous.

On one of my previous visits to the Hardy farm, I had halloed her father in from one of the fields. They had come walking in together, each holding a feed bucket for the young calves, Anne's free hand holding her father's. Their faces were a study—Lem's old and gnarled and faintly bemused as he watched the path, and Anne's alive and animated as she talked, her hand swinging his back and forth. She was telling him a story—that much was obvious. And telling it with great enjoyment, while he listened, more amused—I guessed—by her enthusiasm than by whatever literary tale she was telling.

She had spent a year in college, but there was still money left in her savings account. With what money she had, she purchased a quality male llama and a pregnant female. Lem Hardy had been slow to warm up to the idea of llamas on the farm. But for Anne's sake, he and his three sons had put up the money for a second female llama.

Money put in trust for her by her mother had enabled her, when she turned twenty-one, to purchase two more females. And the humane society from Columbia, South Carolina, had called her and asked her to take an aged female llama, half-blind, that had been donated from the estate of an eccentric with a taste for exotic animals.

The old llama, named Crackers, was about the ugliest llama you ever saw, but also the most interesting. Unlike her aloof colleagues, she wanted to meet every person who stepped into the pasture and to get well acquainted. The fact that she had cataracts in both eyes complicated this. She had to get her face eye to eye with people to see them. She had been known, in her eagerness to meet people, to knock them right over.

I pulled up the long dirt driveway at the Hardy's cattle farm. Anne's three brothers, Billy Bob, Bo, and Jefferson Davis, all waved from the rail fence where they'd perched to swig cold RC's on their morning break.

It was warm and humid, with nothing much going on around the farm. Through the rearview mirror, I saw them one at a time hop off the fence and wander after me. Lem had called the store to place an order and had asked me to come out and get a blood sample from Snow Queen, Anne's white llama.

Lem or any of the boys could take blood samples from a cow, and they kept syringes and equipment on hand to administer inoculations to their cattle. But llamas are harder to "nick," as Lem would say. Getting through all the wool is one problem, but what really makes it bad is that the neck is about the only place on a llama where a vein is accessible. The esophagus is also accessible there, complicating matters. And the hide is about a quarter of an inch thick.

Getting a blood sample from two of Anne's females had taken me an hour the last time I'd tried. A good part of that time had been spent simply trying to restrain them. The restraining chute purchased for just such situations had proved too flimsy.

I did not feel confident about this. Even though I had borrowed articles and pamphlets from Anne about llama anatomy and physiology, I really didn't feel competent to do much for them. Even getting blood seemed a difficult and tedious job. And now it looked like I was going to have an audience. I pulled up to the farmhouse and parked.

Whenever my hero, Wagner Nesbitt, ended up with an audience, he also evidenced nervousness. But Nesbitt always managed to pull off success by some stroke of luck or even humor. The cows often helped him out by reacting quickly to the shots he gave them or by obligingly spitting out infected T.B. phlegm just as he scratched his head in wonder.

Things like that didn't happen to me. Anyway, I knew nothing lucky was going to happen to me today.

I stuffed a bottle of isopropyl alcohol into one pocket and two capped syringes into the other.

"Thought we might watch and get the hang of them things," Billy Bob said as he and the others strolled up to the car.

"Of course," I told him. "The bags are in the car; we'd better get them first."

He nodded his head and flipped a hand at Bo and Jefferson Davis. Billy Bob was eldest and often gave the orders to his brothers. They never argued, at least not in front of me. The two younger Hardys obediently unloaded the feed sacks for me.

We wandered out to the llamas' pasture, called the "goat field" by all the male Hardys. Lem Hardy never called the llamas anything other than "them goats" or "Anne's goats"; at least that was their name to all outsiders.

Lem himself joined us, and the procession followed the fence line all the way out to the small gray barn where Anne waited with Snow Queen.

"Good morning, Jim," she called, and then turned and smiled at her father. "Daddy, will you give us a hand? You don't mind?"

"Not a bit, Pudd'n," he said. "You don't want to try the chute agin?"

"I would if it were Crackers, but Snow Queen jumped so much last time I thought she might break a leg or hurt herself."

He nodded and spit out a squirt of tobacco juice onto the long fescue. "Well, let's do it, then. Shorten up that lead on the halter, Pudd. Billy Bob, you git 'round here, and Bo and Jefferson Davis, you two git that halter and don't you budge, y'hear?"

They made their bodies a wall against Snow Queen. Anne got her arms around the llama's neck and talked to her quietly.

Lem kept his hips up against Snow Queen, but he used his hands to help me get the sample site disinfected. He held the syringe while I probed around the wool on Snow's neck. She didn't like all this attention and sensed that something was coming.

"Easy, girl," I told her. "It won't last a minute if I can find the right spot."

I thought I had it and even felt the surge of triumph that Wagner Nesbitt had so well described. "Just to the right of the windpipe—my right," I said for the benefit of the audience. I slipped in the needle. It pierced the tough llama hide with a slight thrust that made Anne wince and sent a quiver through Snow.

"Almost done," I murmured, but Jefferson Davis grinned and glanced at Bo. No blood had pushed up against the plunger. I probed as long as I dared and then withdrew the needle.

A line of drool ran off Snow Queen's lip. She was nervous. This session had no meaning to her, and there was no way to help her understand it would soon be over.

"Try again," I said hoarsely. I felt with my fingers, located the vein, applied pressure for what seemed like minutes in order to distend the vein, then plunged the needle in. Snow Queen quivered and tried to back away.

"Steady," Lem said. I explored with the needle while following her movements, and finally withdrew the syringe. No blood.

"She's trembling," Anne said. I nearly winced on that remark from Anne.

"I thought I had it," I said. It sounded like an excuse.

"Tricky thing on these animals," Jefferson Davis said. Lem nodded, but the other two men kept their faces steady, as though concentrating on keeping Snow Queen steady.

"This for a pregnancy test?" I asked as we let the llama rest a minute. I wiped off the needle with the disinfectant.

"Yes," Anne said.

She had her pale red hair tied back in a long braid, but a film of perspiration had dampened her face and neck. She was suffering right along with the llama.

"I'll try again," I said, "but if I don't get it, we'll have to postpone it to another day."

"Yes," Anne said briefly, intent on Snow Queen's anxiety.

I tried again, and again the needle remained empty. My teeth clamped tight in frustration. This was no way to impress future clients, and it was certainly no way to win Anne's confidence.

"That's it," she said.

"Maybe once more on the other side," I said. Sweat trickled down my neck into the back of my shirt.

"One more won't hurt," Lem said.

Anne's lips pressed together, but she didn't contradict him. I wanted to try again, so with a nod I tried the other side. Again I was sure that I had it, and again the needle stood empty in Snow's neck.

"Take it out," Anne said. "She can feel it, poor thing."

I obeyed her. The men released Snow Queen, stepped back, and wiped sweat from their faces.

"You'd better set her loose," I said lamely. Anne unsnapped the lead, and Snow Queen gratefully trotted away to join the herd.

"Well, young man, come in anyway and have a drink," Lem said. "Uh oh, watch out!"

We looked up to see Crackers. She was terribly undershot, even for a llama, and she was almost hairless on the face and neck. She walked straight for us, chin thrust out, dim eyes and huffing nostrils trying to pick out who was an everyday person and who was a visitor.

"Watch it, Vet, she's onto ya," Lem said.

I warded her off with an arm. Her breath came in and out with short puffs as she tried to get scent of me.

"Easy does it, Crackers," I said. She was insistent and tried to push past my arm.

"Oh, silly old maid. Bad girl!" Anne exclaimed, and pulled her away. "Behave, Animal Crackers!"

"Watch out, she'll knock you down," Lem said as the old llama followed us again.

"Shoo her off, Jeff, she's a nuisance to Sissy," Billy Bob said.

Anne shot a sideways glance at Billy Bob, and he grinned at her. "Sissy" apparently was their pet name for her.

Jefferson Davis pushed the llama away (there was no point in waving his arms at her— she wouldn't have seen them) and gave her a slap on the rump. Crackers at last retreated.

After failing at such a simple task, I didn't have the heart to go into the Hardys' kitchen. I told Lem that I was expected back at the store.

"Jack likes his lunch early; I'd better get back," I said as we reached my car. I glanced at Anne. "I'm sorry about the blood sample."

"Next time," she said, and she smiled.

"They're odd little goats," Lem added.

"Hey, Vet, if you see a black cat with a limp like, can you catch 'im for us?" Jeff Davis asked.

"Certainly. What's wrong? Cut himself?" I asked.

"He's our barn cat," Anne told me. "We think that he's got a band on his foot. An elastic band or string."

"Wire, maybe," Jeff Davis added.

"I wonder how he got into that?" I asked.

"Somebody put it on him," Anne said with a grimace. "A joke, I guess. Somebody's idea of a joke."

"Cat won't let anyone get close, though," Jeff Davis added. "Can't git it off him."

"I'll keep an eye out for him," I promised. I opened the car door and looked at Anne. I knew the look was sheepish. I felt like an idiot. "Goodbye. Sorry," I said.

3 - Rumors of a Ghost

The last vet who had tried to start a practice in Horse Creek Valley had left in a hurry. While hiking up in the pines and sand on a quest to sight pheasant, he had stumbled onto a knot of farmers all grouped around a steel vat.

"Gentlemen, is this your sorghum mill? I've never seen one before!" he exclaimed, and he scrambled down to join them.

There were other things he had never seen before. They sent him scurrying back into the trees with a load of birdshot. According to the story I heard, several of the pellets hit him direct in the backside. As soon as he was able to sit again, he climbed right into his car and drove away. North. All the way back to Pittsburgh.

That had been ten years ago.

As for me, I adopted a policy never to hike in the pines.

The after-lunch crowd kept the feed store busy in the afternoon. Jack gave me a half hour for lunch while he and the two part-time boys took care of the work up front.

He came into the back just as I cleared up my sandwich papers.

"Still a crowd?" I asked.

"Slowing down, no rush," he told me. "Sales ain't where they was this time last year. That's for sure. No need to hurry your lunch. Them jaw flappers'll be hanging around till supper."

I sat back down at the card table. We had an old Mr. Coffee set up, and I poured out a cup. He took it with a nod of thanks, and I poured one for myself.

"You looked 'bout as low as a snake's chin in a wheel rut when you came in," he observed.

"Couldn't get blood out of a llama," I told him.

"Everything goes wrong in front of a purty gal," he added.

"Not to mention her three brothers and father," I told him.

Jack actually chuckled. "Gave 'em a show, huh?"

"Yeah."

He drained the steaming coffee with one huge draught and tossed the cup in the trash. Without looking at me he said, "Every decent man from here to the Aiken County line wants to marry Anne Hardy—including some what's already married. And the ones that ain't decent wish they was when they see her. You're aiming high, Jim."

"I know," I said.

"And y'know, she don't date much. One to a customer at the most."

"I didn't know that," I said.

He nodded. "Had a real rich fella from those nice houses offa 278 take her to dinner. Thought she'd've made a nice match, y'know? Never have to work, have a nice house, lotta kids, keep up with her church work. But no, she never went with him again."

"Money's not all that important to Anne," I said.

He raised his grizzled eyebrows in agreement to the obvious. "Had a preacher boy ask her out, too. Well, 'bout a dozen of them at least. Same story." Jack tapped a cigarette out of the pack he kept in his shirt pocket. "You'd better go mind the register, Jim. There's other girls than Anne Hardy. I think you better keep an eye out."

I went out front. A half dozen men stood around the back aisle, talking. A few were perched comfortably enough on the fifty-pound bags of fertilizer.

"Hey, Vet," some called, while others called me by name. The part-time boys were straightening up. It was the afternoon lull. I wished for a vet call, but none came. I wanted to work and work hard, to forget those useless thrusts with the needle into Snow Queen's neck.

Talk turned from crops and cattle to local gossip.

"Hey, Vet, heard 'bout the squaw yet?" Howie Dugan asked me. "She's back agin."

"Been out late nights, Vet?" someone else asked me.

"Squaw?" I asked.

"Walks along with a white deer," Howie told me.

Just then Jack came out of the back. "Ya'll talkin' 'bout that again?" he complained. "Same story was goin' around when I was Jim's age." He shot a glance at me. "Story pops up agin every few years. Don't mind it."

"Now, hey, Jack," Davey Miller said. "My old dad saw her himself."

"When, Davey?" Jack asked.

"Oh, 'bout eight, ten years ago."

"Sure, and after a night by the creek, right, fishing for minnows in the moonshine?"

"Aw, go on, my dad's sober. He's a deacon, ain't he?"

"Everybody's a deacon," I mumbled. Horse Creek Valley Baptist Church had 100 members and 37 deacons. Jack was the only one who heard me, and he shot me a glance of agreement with my sarcasm.

"Say what, Vet?" Davey asked.

"What's the story behind the squaw?" I said.

"Folks say way back this Indian gal was a medicine woman—had the spirit of the deer," Howie Dugan told me. "When the Indians had to move out, she said she wouldn't go. She settled in Horse Creek Valley to mourn for her people. Seemed she knew ahead of time they was in for a bad time."

"What happened to her?" I asked.

Howie shrugged. "The white man never caught her. Reckon she just died, finally."

"No, that's not all of it," Jack said. "Howie Dugan, I don't even believe the story, and I know it better than you do."

Davey Miller and several others nodded judicially. Jack glanced at me. "She swore she'd wait for her people to come back. The spirit of the deer would keep her tied to the valley. So folks say they see her at night, an' sometimes the deer's with her. They're waitin' for their people to come back."

"You might see her yourself, Vet, some night on a call," Howie told me.

"He'll only see her after he's had a few," Jack said. "And he don't drink."

4 - The Squaw

The phone shrilled in the darkness. With my hand I groped over the nightstand, knocked over the alarm clock, and at last found the receiver.

"Hello," I gasped.

"James?"

"Yes."

"Lem Hardy. Got a job to do on a calf in a tight cow. C'n you give me a hand? No one here with me but Anne."

"I'll be right there, Lem."

I sat up and waited a second until my head cleared. My clothes were thrown around the room, and I groped for them a piece at a time without turning on the light.

I rented rooms in an old boarding house in Aiken. It was rather quiet there on Saturday nights—most of the other tenants went out.

I'd gone to bed early—before ten—and now it felt as though dawn could not be far off. But when I reeled my alarm clock up by its cord, the luminous face told me that it was only half past midnight.

My model vet, Wagner Nesbitt, could get up on a night call and maintain his doze all the way out to his patient. I couldn't get the hang of that, yet. Once my head got upright for a few minutes, I woke up.

The night was warm and alive with the peaceful noises of crickets and peepers.

I rode out with the window down and wondered what my chances would be of a few minutes' talk with Anne. Jack's warning hung over me like a cloud of gloom. Asking Anne out for a conventional date would be a bad plan. The best way to win her seemed to be by a series of chance and casual meetings.

I hardly paid attention to the quiet roads as I pulled off Highway 19 and onto the back roads of the Valley. It was tempting to simply floor it and get to the farm as quickly as possible. But a lot of the bar patrons would be making their ways home. I pulled up to a stop sign, came to a stop, and was just rolling forward when I saw something at the very edge of my headlights' glare.

It was a shape just inside the fringe of pine trees along the road. It was two shapes. I hit the brakes and tried to turn to get the headlights to sweep the side of the road.

But there was nothing there. I realized that my heart was beating hard against my ribs. In the brief second of my glimpse, I had seen dark braids on the one shadow, and the other had disappeared with a flash of white.

After a moment's futile stare, I backed up and continued up the road.

Lem didn't have electric lights in the barn where he and the cow were trying to bring a calf into the world. As I approached through the pasture, I saw the glow from a coal miner's lantern shine onto the grass through the cracks in the walls. It was a long walk through the dark pasture, and I spent most of it wondering exactly what the Indian squaw's attitude toward the white man would be, now that she'd had a hundred years or so to think about it.

But the minute that I walked into the dim, tumbledown barn, I forgot about what I'd seen out in the pines. Anne was there.

"Hello, Anne," I said.

"Ho, James, it's a good thing you're here!" Lem called

from behind the cow. "Come gimme a hand."

I threw off my jacket and shirt, disinfected my hand and forearm, donned an exam sleeve, and smeared some lubricating jelly onto my gloved hand and arm.

"She's awful boney," Lem gasped as he shuffled aside to relax his legs. The cow was on her feet, snubbed to a ring in the wall. Lem had already tied up her tail and scrubbed up her backside with soap and water. Two tiny legs protruded from the vulva.

I gently inserted my hand into the cow.

"How long has she been straining?" I asked.

"I found her an hour ago, and the water had broke," he said. "She's premature. Calf's feet are comin' out straight, but I can't feel a head."

The pelvis was small, but I still had reason to hope that the calf would be small, too, since it was early.

"Whaddaya think, boy?" he asked.

"The head's turned away," I told him. "I think she's got room for it to come through if we can bring the head toward us."

"Yup, I figured. She's pushing okay—so far."

"Yes. I don't think she's been in labor more than a couple of hours," I told him. "There's not much sign of severe distress."

"Good. Well, we ought to be able to handle this. Anney, dear, you don't have t'stay out here, if you'd rather go t'the house."

"Oh, I don't mind," she told him. I glanced at her and smiled briefly, a smile like any vet would give to a cheering section. A lifetime on a farm had not jaded Anne's keen interest in farm life. And working alongside of Lem, I didn't feel so self-conscious.

For one thing, I knew that Lem had really needed only another pair of hands and perhaps an agreement. I knew perfectly well that if Lem had wanted genuine veterinary assistance, he would have called one of the "real" vets from over in Augusta. He asked my advice as we worked, but at every step I only agreed with him or else provided the appropriate medical term. But he stepped back when I inserted my hand again into the cow. While I found and carefully repositioned the head, Lem looped the chains around the calf's forelegs. I guided the head as Lem gently applied traction on the chains.

The cow gave a hard push, and the bald face appeared. "Looks like a diver, don't it?" Lem chuckled. With a few more pushes from the cow, we eased the new little creature into the world. The calf was alive.

"Well, now," Lem laughed while I dried it off. Anne came forward to help. She bent down near me, and I could smell a clean, slightly soapy, slightly perfumed scent from her hair. She was so intent on the calf that I just watched her slim hands deftly rub circulation into it.

She had donned a pair of Bo's work overalls that were way too big for her, perhaps with an eye to stepping in and assisting if I had failed to come. Under the overalls she wore a pale green blouse, checked. The odd combination of her neatly done-up hair, the womanly blouse, and the rough, droopy overalls that hung from her shoulders and had to be tied at the waist with a length of rope somehow made her even more delightful to look at. She was wonderfully naive about her own beauty—conscious, I thought, of being sweet to the eye and attractive, but unconscious of her ability to turn male heads and keep them turned.

"Been an hour and a half, Jim!" Lem boomed. I nearly jumped out of my skin. I had forgotten him, and I'd been staring at Anne in a kind of reverie.

I glanced at Lem. "You two deserve the lantern," he added. "I'll go 'long first and put coffee on while you finish here."

"We're so grateful to you for coming out, Jim," Anne said. After I had iodined the navel, we lay the calf near its mother, who nosed it over from head to tail, while it made its first attempt at trying to rise to its feet.

"Oh, it's nothing," I told her. "Your father knows as much about calving as any vet, I think. I learn a lot just watching him. He's a calm one, isn't he? Nothing throws him."

She smiled. After a moment she said, "Not much, anyway. But Dad learns to farm every day of his life. He never stops learning."

"Was it his idea for you to pick up that year in agricultural school?" I asked.

Anne looked startled. I'd struck a nerve. "Well, not really," she said. "It didn't go over well. We'd better go."

I took the lamp and collected my things. Anne was silent on the walk back through the pasture.

At last I said, "Well, you know, college isn't for everybody. And course titles don't ensure a successful farm."

She didn't answer me. The light wasn't good, but I thought that she looked worried or upset in some way. The rest of the walk was silent.

As soon as we got into the old farmhouse, Anne said, "Thank you for your help. I think I'll say goodnight now. It's nearly three." And she went up the back steps, leaving me alone in the hall.

Lem had coffee ready. "Where's Anne?" he asked.

"Gone to bed," I said, and sat down.

He offered no other comment but talked on cheerily about the cows, the warm spring, the price of tobacco. Hard-bitten as he was, Lem was a good host. He brought out pie and sliced turkey, bread, cheese, and mustard.

While we were eating, I heard a truck pull up. Doors slammed, and after another minute or two, the three Hardy brothers came stumping in.

"Whoo-whee, Pa!" Bo yelled. "What you doin' up? Howdy, Big Jim!"

"Howdy, Bo," I said.

"You boys hush. Sissy's in bed," Lem told them.

Billy Bob and Bo came clattering into the kitchen while Jeff went on into the hall bathroom. There was a loud noise of water from the faucet crashing into the bathtub.

"That fool's takin' a bath!" Billy Bob said with a giggle. He and Bo went into gales of suppressed laughter.

"Looks like you two could do with some coffee," Lem told them.

Billy Bob waved away the offer. "Oh, Daddy, Howie Dugan's done seen the ghost! You shoulda heard him. He seen it tonight on his way over from t'other side of Aiken."

"The more that boy drank, the bigger and wilder that squaw got," Bo added. Both of them broke into laughter.

I heard Jeff Davis land in the bathtub with a plop and a splash. Billy Bob and Bo broke out laughing again.

Nobody noticed that my smile was glued on. Somehow I had offended Anne, offended her right after having made my one and only good impression on her. The happy triumph of the work I'd done in the barn had turned into a ball of lead in my stomach.

5 - Sunday

In church the next morning, the five Hardys sat in a solid and quiet row. The three boys, then Anne, then her father. None of the three seemed especially hung over. No matter how hard or how late they partied on Saturday nights, Lem had them in church on Sunday morning, lined up like Sunday school children. I wondered if he was hoping that church would eventually tame them.

I watched the back of Anne's head and thought about how much she differed from them—in everything. Lem seemed more able to appreciate her than her brothers did. I wondered why college hadn't worked out for her. It seemed impossible that Anne couldn't have passed the courses. She was sensitive, intelligent, and a hard worker. She spoke much more carefully than most people, as though very conscious of good grammar. Surely education meant a lot to her.

After the invitation and final hymn, I hurried to get out of the pew and leave church. I didn't want another awkward scene with her.

But Billy Bob, Bo, and Jefferson Davis shouldered their way down the aisle in a hurry for their Sunday dinner. I was obliged to wait until they passed. And then I found myself face to face with Anne.

She smiled up at me. "Good morning, Jim. I hope you got some rest after your late night."

"Thank you," I said. "How about you?"

She nodded, and the slightest blush tinted her cheeks. The boys wanted her and Lem to hurry, so they went on.

The feed store was closed Sundays. The first day of the week was always a quiet one in Horse Creek Valley. I decided to do some walking in the early afternoon. Mindful of the misadventures of the last vet, I drove up toward the northeast end of the valley, closer to North Augusta and Clearwater.

My dusty old car climbed higher and higher as it brought me up to the very lip of the valley. The road became a single lane, cut like a gash between high red banks. I passed a huddle of wooden frame houses and realized that I was in a black section of Horse Creek Valley.

The families sat on the porches of the unair-conditioned frame houses. Nobody paid especial notice of me, but I watched them thoughtfully as I drove by.

I don't think that Horse Creek Valley had ever seen racial violence between blacks and whites. The KKK had no history there. There had never been rumors of trouble from the blacks. Neither side had been interested in confrontation. I don't suppose that the freedom riders had even penetrated it. After all, what would they have found? Neither whites nor blacks had wanted to intermingle with the other. They had wanted peace.

But now it was the last part of the twentieth century. There was still no intermingling. Black men and white men might work side by side in town, but they continued their private lives at Horse Creek Valley in complete separation. And there was still peace, but no understanding, and no respect.

The old car climbed farther, past a section of roomy brick houses. Television antennae sprouted at each chimney, and I passed an array of Toyota Celicas and Nissan Sentras and other mid-sized cars. Even the more affluent blacks lived here. I wondered if they chose to or were forced to. Laws had changed, but legal changes were no good unless attitudes changed.

At last the narrow pavement ended, and I trundled over a red clay road, past a cemetery. There were more wood frame houses ahead. This time, the families on the stoops turned and watched me come. I felt self-conscious and tried to look nonchalant. The parents went on talking, but the children continued to stare. And somehow I knew, even though the adults had assumed a nonchalance equal to my own, that they were wondering who the heck I was and what I was doing wedging my huge old car between the banks of dirt.

My car windows were all down because of the hot day. I felt curiously exposed, especially when I saw that around the bend there were more houses, not fewer. And furthermore, the road dead-ended. I pulled up and stopped in front of a huge bank of dirt.

I felt like a fool. A big, white, out-of-place fool. There was nothing to do but try to pilot that huge car back and forth in pitiful arcs until I got it turned.

I began this operation. By now, many of the adults had given up their studied nonchalance. They watched with puzzled amusement. I forgot all my philosophical regrets. I was out of place and wanted to get back to a more familiar society.

I had nearly gotten the car back around when I noticed a man pop out of one of the houses. He came sprinting across the clumpy grass and up the dusty road. He ran right up to the car and slapped his hands on the sill.

"You the vet?" he asked.

I realized that I'd been holding my breath. "Yes," I told him. "Can I help you?"

"The dog's been chewed to pieces by varmints. She came in this morning but I can't git the wounds stanched."

"I'll come right up," I said. At least it looked as though

I had some purpose here.

I pulled up and parked on the grass alongside the road. I had suture in the car as well as other veterinary supplies. I grabbed what I needed and followed him into the house. The front room was furnished modestly. A picture of Jesus hung on one wall. The dog lay in a box in the kitchen. She was a long-haired bitch of medium height but finely boned. Breed was anyone's guess. I would have judged her to have some spaniel in her, and border collie, perhaps. A good, reliable mutt and a family dog.

I felt for broken bones. Her right forefoot had been caught in an animal's mouth. There wasn't much of a puncture, but it was tender for her. At last I decided that it wasn't broken, only bruised where the jaws had closed on it.

I peeled back an eyelid. It was pale pink.

She was torn up in plenty of places, but the only bad gash was on her right side, along her belly. She would need a general anesthetic before I could repair the wound. I injected some rompun plus ketamine into a vein.

"Much deeper and this would have disemboweled her," I said. I clipped away hair and thoroughly cleansed the wound with an antiseptic solution. Muscle had been torn, but I didn't suspect internal bleeding. Nevertheless, I had to do a lot of piecework in order to suture the torn edges of the muscle together. I was glad when, at last, I was able to close the wound. I finished up by giving her a shot of antibiotics.

"This wasn't varmints, Mr. . . . uh, Mr. . . . ."

"Didee." He smiled at me and added, "Jedidiah. But they call me Didee for short."

"Well, Didee," and I nodded at him, "this wasn't varmints. She was mauled by other dogs. A pack of them, I would say."

"Dang me," he shook his head. "There's more wild dogs

up here than you could count, Vet."

"I'll give her a shot against rabies, but if one of her attackers carried it . . ."

He shook his head. "I'll keep an eye on her, but I think they're just wild cusses. They wouldn't keep living and breeding like they do if they was mad."

Meanwhile, several members of Didee's household wandered in and stood behind us, trying to get a look.

"She'll need quiet and care for a few days," I told him. "Keep her warm at night. I think I'll stop up tomorrow night, if you don't mind, just to see how she's doing."

"You'd be very welcome," Didee said.

We stood up with some difficulty. I realized then that my shirt had stuck to my back. My knees and shoulders were stiff. The sunlight that had been so powerful now slanted comfortably through the back windows.

"What do I owe you?" Didee asked.

"Oh, nothing," I said. "I'm not in practice, Didee. My boss gets my supplies for me. I'm good advertising for him."

He nodded. "I thought you'd been behind the counter at the feed and seed store. But I'd seen your car at the farms, too. It was good luck you came up this way today."

I gulped. "Yes, I guess it was."

I shot a glance at my watch. There was no way I'd get to the evening service at church. Would Anne wonder where I was?

"Now look! I kep' you here most of the afternoon," he began, worried.

"No, no, it's all right," I said. "I was just thinking of someone . . . but . . . it's not that I had an engagement. It's fine."

"Would you stay for supper, then?" he asked.

The offer startled me. But I said, "Yes, thank you. That'll give me a chance to see how she wakes up after the anesthesia."

We went out on the front porch, where the shade had increased. With the evening coolness coming on, most of the neighborhood children were on their bicycles or racing around on foot. The adults had gone inside.

Didee was Jack's age, if not older. He was at least ten years older than Cirrell, his wife. They had three children, none of them yet teenagers.

Cirrell brought us cold Pepsi to drink. We chatted about local news, the weather, and the chances for the peach harvest. What I really wanted was for Didee just to tell me about himself, his life, what it was like to be a black man in Horse Creek Valley.

But I didn't think I knew him well enough to ask him. And yet I felt the loss of not asking. I'd heard black militants talk about their lives, and I'd heard black politicians, but I'd never heard a calm, ordinary black person talk about his life.

Cirrell called us in to dinner: pork ribs, macaroni and cheese, and a dish of bitter greens that I took to be dandelion, but Didee called it "poke."

The children ate in a hurry and raced out again to take advantage of an hour more to play.

Cirrell had asked me about the dog, but she stayed quiet for the most part; I think that she was as curious about how I felt among them as I was about them and what they thought.

But Didee was at ease. He took me out walking in his "garden," a two-acre lot nearby where he planted vegetables. Afterward we went and looked over the cemetery.

"Got cousins in here," he told me, "and an uncle. He got killed in Vietnam. One of the first black men I ever knowed who figured to make the Army a career. But he was too dang conscientious. Picked the worst places to go. He volunteered for Vietnam. Oh, that boy had such plans . . ."

He shook his head, and we would have walked away, but I heard something. I stopped. "What's that, Didee?" It sounded like a distant singing.

He cocked an eyebrow at me. "It's the squaw. Ain't you heard her before? She been singin' since the sun went on the wane."

"You've heard her for that long?" I asked.

"Sure," he shrugged, "but then, I know how t' listen."

He started back for the house, and I followed him. "You mean you believe in the squaw and her doe?"

"Nah, that part about the doe is a' invention. But the squaw's been aroun' a century."

I couldn't hear the singing any more. I didn't know what to say or think. We came back up the road.

"Some folks," Didee said, "forget to listen to the land. Ain't you heard that poet say we were the land's before the land was ours?"

"Frost," I said.

"He was right," Didee smiled. "I'm a Christian man, Vet, or a Baptist anyway. But I know the earth has her secrets. I just listen for them, that's all. There's a lot of mystery locked up in this here valley, and I don't mean hidden stills or shallow graves." He held out his hand. "See you tomorrow."

"Thank you, Didee. I'll see you then."

We shook hands, and I climbed into the car.

6 - More Mishaps

Didee was not a regular customer of Jack's, so I wasn't sure how Jack would feel about my taking the time to drive up and visit the dog.

But when I came in, I found Jack hiding some important news under his crusty exterior. We looked at each other, and he raised his grizzled eyebrows and then turned away.

"What's up?" I asked.

"What do you mean, 'What's up?'" he asked. "It's Monday morning, and we've got new inventory stacked all the way out the back door. Let's take care of it."

"Sure."

"Oh, and Lem Hardy called. Said that one of Anne's goats needs his teeth clipped and could you do it." He passed into the back room. I followed him.

"What did you tell him?"

Jack put his head back around the corner. "That if we finished by ten I'd let you go. So you'd better get a fire lit and get back here, boy."

We had an hour to pack things away before the store opened at nine. As we tossed the heavy sacks into their places, I said, "I thought you wanted me to get over Anne."

Lem had a cigarette hanging off his bottom lip. Without looking up, he said, "I do, but if you still mean to get her as a wife, I'll give you a hand when I can. Soon as she shoots you down once and for all, we'll get to work finding you someone else. Don't you want a gal with college behind her, Jim? Might get dull bein' married to a farmer's daughter. What would you talk about?"

"Anne's as smart and refined as any woman I graduated with," I told him.

"Sure."

"Look, Jack, why did Anne only go for one year?" I asked. "I bet you know."

He straightened up, took the cigarette out of his mouth, and exhaled. "Sure, I know," he said. "It still hurts her, poor gal."

"Well?"

"Her mama's dying request was for Lem to let Anne go to school, you know. And she willed Anne enough money to make a good start anyway."

"The money that Anne used to buy the llamas?" I asked.

"Yup. See, Anne started in something, you know, not farming or technical."

"Liberal arts," I said.

"Yeah. But her daddy was so broke up about her mama's death. And with Anne gone, too, he turned right miserable. The three boys blamed Anne. So she switched over to agriculture after one semester. I reckon she did it to please them. But there wasn't any pleasin' 'em till she was home. Lem gave her that pasture. And she went out and bought the llamas." He gave a chuckle of admiration and pity. "Llamas in Horse Creek Valley! She had to be different. But at least it was something new and exciting for her. Something to learn." He shook his head. "Poor girl."

That explained Anne's behavior on Saturday night. I really had struck a nerve.

"Is she unhappy, Jack?" I asked.

"Anne's happy because she's just a happy gal," he told me. "She'll manage. She always has. But she wanted to go to college. And her mama wanted her to go, too."

We went back to work. Jack kept glancing at me every

few minutes, but at last he changed the subject. "Howie Dugan saw the squaw Saturday night. Couple o' high school kids saw it Sunday night."

"On Sunday night?" I asked. "Where?"

"Over by Aiken, same place as Howie'd seen it the night before."

That would be close to where I'd seen it on Friday night.

"What time?" I asked.

"Oh, just at dusk," he told me.

Yet I'd heard the squaw on Sunday at dusk clear across the valley from Aiken.

"You don't really believe all them nugget heads, do you, Jim?" he asked.

"Well, it seems like a lot of them have seen it," I said.

"Aw, high school kids'll see anything. And if Howie Dugan rolled his brains around and shook 'em out, he wouldn't get high enough to crap out."

"I was up by North Augusta last night," I said to change the subject.

"Oh?"

"Up by the water tower," I added.

"Out where the niggers live?" he asked.

I didn't say anything else. There wasn't any point in asking, and I wasn't going to defend either Didee or myself. I'd go up after work. But Jack surprised me.

"The blacks, I mean?" he asked.

"Yes," I told him. I didn't go into the whole story. I just said, "I have a friend up there with a dog that's been hurt. I'd like to get off early, if I can, to check on it."

"Sure, I'll let you go," Jack said.

"Thanks."

Jack didn't have many black customers, so he knew this wouldn't make us any money. "What happened to the dog?" he asked.

"Run down by a pack," I told him. "It got away, but it was chewed up plenty."

"Good dog?"

"Just a mutt bitch, but I'm sure he uses it for hunting and as a family dog."

"I've seen many a man cry worse over losin' a good bitch than his own wife," Jack said. "But that pack's bad news. Wild wolves or coyotes ain't a peck on dogs gone wild. They'll kill dogs, livestock, and humans to boot." He glanced at me and lifted his gray eyebrows, "Not to mention llamas. If I was your black friend, I'd get me a gun and fix their tails."

I had the materials needed to saw the teeth off of Anne's stud, Robert E. Lee. Llamas don't have teeth on their upper jaws in front. Their upper palate is hard, and mastication occurs using the back teeth. But males do have six "fighting teeth" that they use on other males. These teeth usually grow in, three on each side, by the time the male llama is two or three. A powerful and angry male can make a gelding out of a younger male or do enough damage to seriously injure even full-grown males. Even females can be injured by an overly aggressive male during the mating ritual.

I took some obstetrical wire, a few bottles of isopropyl alcohol, two syringes, and a squirt bottle.

The day had been cloudy at the start, and by the time I got out on the road, the highway and landscape looked as though someone had stretched gray gauze across it. A misty rain fell, the kind that obscures the windshield no matter where you set the wiper speed.

The Hardy boys were at work at various places on the farm, but Lem and Anne accompanied me out to the llama pasture.

"I think that we can use the restraining chute on Robert E. Lee," Anne told me. "He's got enough sense not to jump at the rails."

"Good. Where is he?"

"In one of the stalls. The restraining chute's in another. I'll bring him in to you."

"All right," I said as I fished out the various materials from my pockets. The first thing to do would be to calculate the dosage on the tranquilizer. The removal would be quick, but would hurt some, and the llama would stand less still for each successive one of the six teeth.

I thought carefully about the amount of drug to use and finally calculated dosage based upon weight, using half the dosage per kilogram I'd use for horses. I could always give more in a second shot if I needed to.

But with me so deep in thought, Lem's call, "Look out, Vet!" came too late.

Something clipped my ear and nearly knocked me over; then it swung around and bumped the back of my head. It was Crackers.

Being nearly blind, she was pleased at having zeroed in on me. She puffed out her breath through her nose and huffed her nostrils back in.

"Crackers, go somewhere else!" I commanded, as I pushed her away.

Lem chuckled. Luckily, I hadn't dropped the needle, but I felt exasperated at being made to look like a fool. "Let's get on with it," I said.

The restraining chute was made of metal poles bolted to a poured concrete surface. The llama stepped between railings that came up to his back on either side. We affixed straps over his back and under his belly to keep him steady and rested his head in a yoke. The walls of the chute closed behind him in a triangle formation so that he couldn't back out. Lem tied his halter to the front of the chute so that he couldn't swing his head.

Robert E. Lee was a pretty calm llama. He had a regal bearing and made a very desirable stud. I think he was too dignified to struggle, especially when he knew he wouldn't win.

"About this rompun dosage," I said, "it's going to be some guesswork. I'll start with a bit of a low dosage and then give more if he fights. All I want to do is relax him a bit."

"Same as a goat dose," Lem told me.

"Well, based on weight, I thought I'd give $\frac{3}{4}$ cc."

He shrugged, but Anne nodded. "Give it a try," she said.

"All right, Robert old boy," I told him while his eyes studied something in the other direction. "This won't hurt—much."

I gave him the injection and waited a few minutes. After his eyes glazed slightly, I propped open his mouth by laying in a short piece of a sawed-off broomstick. I wanted to hurry because, even with a tranquilizer, he'd be uncomfortable.

I started on the left side. Anne held the squirt bottle to rinse out his mouth after each tooth was snapped out. The obstetrical wire was actually used to "saw" each tooth out. By pulling the wire with a quick sawing motion back and forth, I could break the tooth off at the gum in five or six strokes. The friction from the sawing would generate heat, and that's when Anne would need to squirt water to cool his mouth.

After the first tooth snapped off cleanly, I felt Robert E. Lee's jaw moving. "Lem, you'd better keep a hold on that lead," I said. "He's trying to ease his head out."

"Okay, Vet."

His head straightened for a minute or two, but after two more teeth, the front jaw and chin began to slide upward again. I didn't want to nag Lem, but I shot him a glance and said, "Sure you've got it?"

"I'm keepin' it taut, but he's sliding," Lem said.

Anne glanced at Lem and then looked at Robert E. Lee's eyes. They were closed. An oddly human sound came up from the llama's throat and nose.

"Is he snoring?" Anne exclaimed. As if in answer, his muzzle slid up again as his head and legs relaxed.

"Reckon $\frac{3}{4}$ cc was a bit much," Lem said meekly.

"Well, as long as he's upright, let's finish," I said. I had three more teeth to snap out before he got so relaxed that he wouldn't be able to stand. I wondered if anything would ever go right for me at the Hardy farm.

As Robert E. Lee happily snored away, I sawed off the other three teeth while Anne cooled his mouth with the squirt bottle.

By the time I finished, he was starting to sag all over. We moved quickly to release his head and open the chute so that he could ease down without hurting himself. Since he was sleeping, I made the most of it and trimmed his toenails with Anne's and Lem's help. It was not easy with him in the sternal-recumbent position, but we were able to get to them all. I monitored his respiration for awhile to make sure he was okay. Then there was nothing to do but wait for him to wake up. An awkward silence ensued.

I was about to apologize to Anne for knocking out her stud when she exclaimed, "Oh, there he is, the barn cat!" And a sleek black tom darted past us and into the barn. I could see that the right paw was injured. He favored it as he ran, using a quick succession of leaps instead of a cat's usual smooth glide.

"I'll get him," I said, as I ran after him.

Barn Cat obviously had expected human interference. He whisked out of sight into a crevice behind the barn's ladder.

The ladder was an old, gray, makeshift arrangement that had been nailed together and then bolted into the barn wall. It led up into the hay loft.

"Here, kitty kitty, let me see your paw," I said soothingly to him, or rather to the two baleful green eyes that glowed from their hiding place.

Barn Cat hissed a warning. I was hoping that a cat with an injured paw wouldn't be able to scratch effectively, especially the way he was wedged in back there.

I was wrong.

While my hand was still a good ten inches away, Barn Cat leaped out like a black whip, scratched my hand, bit my thumb, and darted three rungs up the ladder.

From that high perch he glared down at me. I shook my smarting hand and looked up at him. One last hiss at me, and then he leaped—somewhat lopsidedly—the rest of the way up into the loft.

Anne hurried in. "Did you get him?"

I shook my head. I was mad but tried to keep it clamped down. Nothing ever went right at the Hardy farm.

"Oh, dear," Anne said, more for the cat's sake than for mine.

"I think this farm has jinxed me," I said. I was trying to say something light, but even to me the words sounded bitter and discouraged.

Just then we heard sounds coming from Robert E. Lee's direction. He was just waking up and had already managed to struggle to his feet. He weaved back and forth around the stall with his lead rope dragging.

"Oh, poor fellow." Anne followed him around the stall, trying to get the lead rope off. She finally caught him, snapped off the lead, and released him to continue his staggering around the stall. Already he was getting more sure-footed, and his eyes had lost a bit of their glaze.

Robert E. Lee was going to be okay, but I wasn't so sure about myself. I just wanted out of there, fast. A llama and a cat, and I looked like a fool to Anne again. I didn't want her pity, or even her encouragement, just then. I just wanted out. So without waiting to say something worse than I had said about being jinxed, I simply told her, "I've got to get back. I'm sorry I couldn't get the cat. 'Bye."

"Did he hurt your hand?" Anne asked.

"Just a scratch. It's nothing. I'd better hurry." I walked away and quickly turned the walk into a fast, determined stride.

7 - A Glimpse of Didee

Didee's end of the valley proved a welcome change that night. On impulse I had stopped at a roadside stand and had picked up strawberries and then a gallon of ice cream at the store.

"Thought this might prolong my stay," I said as I met him on the dusty lawn in front of his house.

"Well, James, you'd always be mighty welcome!" he exclaimed. "Come inside!"

The kids were ready for dessert at a moment's notice. Cirrell smiled a gracious thanks at me and went to prepare the strawberries.

Didee and I took a look at the dog. She was more alert and even slapped her tail against the bottom of the box.

"Looks like she's doing well," I told him.

"Sure is. Say, if you can wait on that dessert, I thought you might take a walk with me," Didee said.

"Certainly. Where?"

"Dog down the street got kilt last night. I'm taking my gun out."

I felt a slight unease. Night wasn't the best time to hunt, but then the pack did its worst damage at night and would be almost impossible to find by day.

"Can't poison 'em," Didee added. "Not without puttin' a lotta huntin' hounds in danger."

"Is it legal?" I asked.

He shrugged and added, "I thought you might like to come along. It's not a job I like to do alone."

"I'll be glad to go with you," I said.

Didee had taken the time to learn the pack's habits and its regular courses. He had only one .22 to take, so I carried the lantern.

The job was not a pleasant one. It's never pleasant to kill animals that were once domesticated. Hunger and need had made them a wild pack, not any innate wickedness.

Didee stationed himself on the edge of a field. Not long after, the pack came gliding into view. There were five of them, and they were chasing game—most likely a rabbit, but perhaps a weasel or opossum.

Didee's gun rang out four times. Two of the pack sprang away and disappeared without giving him much chance. But three fell, of which one still wallowed in agony as we came up closer. Didee ended his misery.

He wiped his forehead with his free hand. "Well, that's done. Let's take them over to the garbage dump. It's just over yonder—one of their favorite haunts."

We dragged them away to the dump—an open, vile-smelling place, unmistakable even at night. I held up the lantern and surveyed piles of rags, old shoes, bits of machinery, and even a couple of old car chassis.

"I could do with a wash," Didee said. "Dang dirty business."

I don't know why the shedding of blood should have drawn us closer together. But on the long walk back to the house, I asked Didee about the lines of separation that were still so rigid in Horse Creek Valley.

He cited a lot of reasons: the cultures themselves were still quite different, and the people felt safer with old ways than with new ways, and family ties kept the whites and blacks going in separate circles.

"Has there ever been fighting?" I asked.

"Oh, sure—," he began, when suddenly he stopped as

though he'd hit a brick wall. "What the thunderation's that!"

I looked around, but it took me a second to realize that we were looking right at the squaw. The white deer stood behind her, partly obscured by her figure. She was within a hundred feet of us. She quickly moved off into the trees.

"It's the squaw!" I whispered.

"If that's a squaw, I'm a squaw!" Didee exclaimed.

"Let's chase her, Didee!"

"With me holdin' a gun?" he asked me. "You'd see violence then for sure. I'd get lynched!"

"Can't you hide it somewhere?"

Didee laughed. "Lookit you. You're worse than a school kid. Go chase her if you want, James. I don't mind."

"No, I'll stay with you," I said. "But how do you know it's not the squaw?"

We resumed our walking.

"'Cause you hear the squaw singin,'" he told me. "I heard her when we first went out, but she's been silent a good while now."

"Well, who could fake the squaw?" I asked. "Who could get a tame white deer to drag along?"

"If it was a deer," he added. "You get a good look at it?"

"No," I admitted. "She keeps it behind her all the time."

"How many times you seen her?" he asked.

"Twice now."

"I b'lieve she's haunting you," he laughed.

"No, I just have a talent for being in the wrong place at the wrong time," I told him, "and for saying the wrong thing when I get there."

"Uh oh," he said, "you ain't happy here?"

"I don't know," I told him. "I guess I'm still kind of an outsider. And I really complicated things by falling for a girl that lives over on the other side of the valley."

"Well, ain't she impressed with you bein' a vet an' all?" he asked.

"No. I keep acting like a dope in front of her," I said.

He glanced over at me and after a minute said, "Maybe you're too hard on yourself."

"I don't think so, Didee."

8 - Calls

Jack expected me to take some cases for the sake of the customers more than for the sake of professionalism. I was pulling out ticks and thorns much more often than delivering weanlings or diagnosing livestock. And there were some calls that put me right out of my ken.

Like the call from Wayne Westerly.

"Hey, is the vet in?"

"This is Jim."

"Oh, hey, Vet. This 'ere's Wayne Westerly. I need some he'p from you. Y'might have to come out."

"What's the trouble?"

Well, I got me this big huge old rat back by the water heater in the house. See, we still polishing things up yet, and the water heater ain't enclosed. He's a big fella."

"Well, that's really odd," I said. "Usually a rat would run at the sight of a person."

"Oh, he cain't run, Vet."

"Is he stuck?"

"Stuck? Heck no! He's dead!"

"Dead?"

"Sure. I shot him. Took one look at him and eased my handgun outta the kitchen drawer and got him on the first shot." A pause. "He's dead, all right."

"I see. Well, Wayne, if he's dead, I'm sure that he can be safely removed. You might want to wear rubber gloves to do the job. Dispose of the gloves, of course. But it's safe."

"Well, it don't seem safe."

"Why not?"

"They's twisted sheet metal all over the corner where he's dead. I skinned open the water heater with the bullet. Tear the fire outta my hands, I imagine."

"Maybe you should try leather gloves."

"And then again, too, he's spattered ever'where. That shot tore him up right good." Another pause. "That's what I get for using a .357 on a rat behind the water heater. But the .22 was clean acrost the house."

"Really, Wayne, I'm not sure what you're asking me."

"Well, you're the vet, ain't you? I thought you'd come gimme a hand and get him outta here before the missus gets home."

Jack, wondering what was taking so long, wandered into the back room. One look at me told him that I was in distress. He mouthed one word at me, "Who?"

I mouthed back the answer, "Wayne Westerly."

"C'n you come out right quick?" Wayne asked.

"Uh, let me check with Jack, Wayne." I covered the phone and looked at Jack. "Say no."

"No," Jack said.

I took the receiver again. "He says no, Wayne."

"Dang it. Oh, well, I guess I better get it done then. Thanks anyway, Vet."

Calls from Wayne usually topped my list of things to avoid, but my prize call came from Howie Dugan himself. But Howie came in person.

I should say that Howie Dugan usually was the butt of everybody's jokes. He was a necessary part of the social structure among the farmers who patronized and hung out at the store, and so there were long periods when they gentled up on him and tried to take him seriously. But the truth was, if they weren't playing jokes on him or stretching his credibility to the limit, he was usually doing it to himself. He was a short, round-bottomed man, whose balding head was usually covered in a feed cap of considerable age and wear.

I had it on good authority that there was no equal to him in carpentry work, hunting skills, or other abilities crucial to the small farm owner. It was mostly in common sense that Howie had missed something.

He came running and bouncing into the store one Saturday afternoon, a small river of blood streaming down from his lip, over his chin, and onto a white terry towel that he clutched up to his face every now and then.

"Vet, Vet!" he exclaimed. "Help me—tell me straight, kin a man get rabies from a lizard bite?"

Without comment, Jack fished the first-aid kit out from under the counter and tossed it to me.

"Rabies?" I asked. "No, it's impossible, but what happened to you? Here, hold still, move that towel."

He obeyed as meekly as a child. His younger brother Buck had come in after him, his face a show of both amusement and concern. I tried to pack gauze around the cut on his lip, but bandaging a lip is no easy thing, and blood continued to flow freely around the gauze. It took me a second to realize that the wound was neither a puncture nor an incisor wound, as I had assumed, but rather an avulsion.

"What in the world happened?" I asked. Other people in the store drifted closer.

"I was working on the porch this morning, gettin' ready for the barbecue today with my family," Howie said through my fingers and the wads of gauze. "An' little bitty Toby from next door brung me over a lizard to look at."

"And it bit you?"

Buck snorted a laugh, and Howie looked a little annoyed. "'Course not! I was tryin' to hurry and git the porch done, and I tol' that scamp I couldn't look at his lizard and to go 'way and leave me 'lone for an hour or two. He just kep' botherin' me, sayin', 'Lookit my lizard, Howie, lookit my lizard! Com'n, Howie, lookit my lizard!'"

"Right pesky," Buck agreed.

I threw down the two bloody wads of gauze and pushed the towel back at him so he could tell the rest of the story without my hands in his mouth.

Howie continued, holding the towel pushed against his lower lip. "So fin'ly he was such a nuisance I yelled, 'Lemme 'lone boy, here's fer yer lizard!' and I plucked up the lizard, bit its darn head off, and throwed it down."

Everybody looked at Howie as though seeing him for the first time.

"You done bit the head off a lizard?" one of the men asked.

"That's what he tells me," Buck affirmed.

"Is that what you mean, can you get rabies from a lizard bite?" I asked him. "From biting a lizard? The answer is still no. But I hope you spit the head out."

He fixed me with another annoyed stare. "Y'think I'd be dumb enough to swallow it?"

"I never thought you'd be dumb enough to bite it off," I admitted.

"Well, that ain't what I come for," he replied, his voice muffled by the towel. "I went over later and 'pologized to Toby for killin' his lizard. He'd cried and run off when I first done it, but I guess by an' by he got to thinkin' about it and had told his daddy. His daddy thought it was funny."

"So then we all come over for the barbecue," Buck said, picking up the tale while Howie pushed the bloody towel to his lip and winced. "Howie told me what he done, but I didn't believe him."

"No, he didn't," Howie affirmed through the towel. "But he believes me now."

"I called ever'body together and told 'em Howie said he'd bit the head off a lizard," Buck added, "and none of them believed it neither. We was all full of beer, an' I guess we picked on him some for sayin' such a thing."

"So I had to prove it, Vet," Howie said. "I went back into the woods by my house and got me another lizard."

Everybody leaned closer. Even Jack looked up from the counter where he'd been studying a catalogue. Howie leaned closer to me to indicate that he'd like another go with a wad of gauze.

While I tried again, he said, "They was all sayin', 'Bite his head off 'm, Howie, go on, bite his head off.' So I took him firm and opened my mouth." On this he pulled away from me to demonstrate by opening his mouth. "An' that little lizard cuss opened his mouth real wide, like this." He opened his mouth in imitation of a lizard's toothless yawn. "So I pulled back, and when I pulled back, he shut his mouth. So I opened up again to bite him, and he went and opened his mouth, like this."

Howie demonstrated again, indicating that as he had pulled the lizard closer, both he and the lizard had been opening their mouths wider and wider, as though in a contest to swallow each other.

"So I pulled back, and he shut his mouth agin, and then Buck commenced to taunting me even more, sayin' that I hadn't ever done that to no lizard nowhere. I knew I had to do it, so I crammed his head into my mouth real quick, only he was too fast for me, and he done latched onto my lip before I got him in."

He pulled the towel against his lip again. "Oh, Vet, it hurt like a door shuttin' on yer finger, only it was my lip. I couldn't help what I done. I just pulled that rascal off as hard as I could, an' he done took a piece o' my lip with him."

"Could you get me some ice from next door?" I asked Buck. Buck nodded and raced out. "We'll try to slow it with cold and pressure," I told Howie. "But a medical doctor would be of more use than me."

"Where 'm I gonna find one of them on a Saturday?" he asked. He had a point.

Buck returned with the ice, and I wrapped it in plastic and then gauze and instructed him to keep it on his lip and talk as little as possible. He nodded with a mournful look at me, and I added, "Don't worry, you can't get rabies from a lizard. It was probably more dangerous for you the first time, when you bit that one's head off, than the second time, when the one bit your lip. From now on I'd advise you to stick to a hamburger diet, Howie."

9 - A Night on the Town

The rest of the week passed quietly enough. I didn't find much point in telling Jack about the squaw that I had seen with Didee. Other reports came in of people having seen it. He scoffed at all of them. I had enough worries without taking on Jack's sarcasm, so I kept quiet.

Friday morning, the three Hardy brothers came in. The store was busy, and I hardly had time to attend to them.

But as I rang up their order, Billy Bob said, "Say, Jim, why'n't you take it easy one night and come on out to supper with us?"

"If your father doesn't mind," I told him.

"No, no. I mean out, boy, out! Not over t' the house."

"Oh, sure," I told him.

"We could pick you up after work tonight," Jefferson Davis said.

"Sure."

"Oyster bar and a few beers. You workin' tomorrow?"

"In the afternoon."

"We'll be by tonight. You been a wallflower too long." He started to walk away, but then he turned back and grinned. "Maybe we'll see the squaw."

The part-time boys came in at noon, and it was my turn to take lunch first. But Jack came in while I was eating.

"What's up?" I asked.

"Not much. Thought I'd get coffee."

"Just made it," I told him.

He poured himself a cup and leaned against the table.

"What'd Jefferson Davis want?" he asked.

"They got some alfalfa pellets."

He nodded, and then he added, "They pickin' you up tonight?"

"Uh huh." I swallowed a big lump of tuna salad and glanced up at Jack.

He tapped out a cigarette and lit it. He puffed away a few times. At last, through a cloud of smoke around his head, he said, "Thought you was a mild-mannered type, Jim."

"I am."

"Them Hardy boys go for wild times, boy."

"Oh, well, I can handle myself."

"Why bother?"

I shrugged, "They're Anne's brothers."

"They play a lot, Jim, but they play mighty rough."

I felt a little irritated with him. "I can take care of myself, Jack."

"Suit yourself. I ain't no puritan, but seems like a boy with all that college crammed in his head can do somethin' better'n pour in a lot of beer on top of it."

I didn't answer him.

After a minute he mashed the cigarette into an ashtray and went back out front.

Anne, I knew, believed in absolute temperance, and I had thought about the issue a lot. I certainly thought that drunkenness was wrong.

But Wagner Nesbitt, my hero, could go to a pub and drink pints all night without ever consuming more than two or three altogether. While his companions, Gilbert and Sullivan Tarnish, especially Sullivan, could quaff down eight to ten pints in the same amount of time. (Wagner must have sipped his.) And sometimes Nesbitt would go out after a night of beers, diagnose a farrowing pig, and administer pitosin.

Of course, Billy Bob, Bo, and Jefferson Davis didn't go out to have "two or three." That wasn't even enough for a warm-up. But I could keep my head. They'd probably need me along anyway to drive them home.

It didn't matter how I reasoned it out. The fact was, I was so lonely and so much an outsider in Horse Creek Valley, that I knew I would go. I would have gone if they'd asked me to a flower show.

As for Anne, I thought it might not be a bad idea to befriend her brothers, all the while showing her that I possessed more genuine restraint and maturity than they. I could sample their lifestyle without bogging down in it.

Jack fussed and fumed the afternoon away and declared that the time was coming on to keep the store open late for spring and summer hours, and if he'd thought of it sooner, he'd have started tonight, and maybe he should anyway.

"Suit yourself," I told him. "But it's going to be lonely working the place by yourself."

Even I was a little concerned over exactly what type of places the Hardy brothers patronized. Bars were more common than churches in Horse Creek Valley, and some of those establishments that dotted Highway 278 were nothing but gutted houses whose walls had been patched and windows boarded over. The management of these places usually advertised their wares by spray painting something straightforward onto the raw wood door like "Bar" or "Cheap Beer Sold Here."

But when the boys came to get me in their huge truck, I saw that they had traded their farm caps for cowboy hats. Billy Bob sported a silk shirt opened to reveal his muscular neck, and Bo and Jeff Davis wore sport shirts. All had on dark designer jeans and fancy boots.

I felt somewhat honored that they had donned their fancier clothes for the occasion. The smell of Vitalis and Lectra Shave was stifling as I climbed in.

"Howdy, Jim!" Billy Bob boomed at me. "Seafood tonight. Sound good?"

"Sure."

"Didn't want to give you too wild a time," he added, "you not seemin' the type."

"Thanks, I guess not," I said.

"Having gone to college and all."

I glanced at him to check the sarcasm, but he was guiding the truck out onto the highway.

"Hot day," Jeff Davis said, tipping up his hat.

"Sure is," I agreed.

We drove over to Augusta, to a brightly lit, fenced-in little place. I didn't know anyone there, but the Hardys were obviously frequent customers.

As soon as we sat down, the waitress brought us a round of draft beer in tall glasses.

"Oysters all around?" she asked.

"Same as usual, lovely lady," Billy Bob said.

She smiled at him and soon returned with our food.

For a while there was only the sound of our eating and drinking.

Billy Bob ordered beer by the pitcher. As the food kept coming—oysters and then peel 'n eat shrimp and, as we kept at it, fried okra, salad, and hushpuppies—he would offer me more to drink. After two huge glasses, I told him I'd had enough.

But the hushpuppies and the sauce for the shrimp made me thirstier and thirstier. Billy Bob would slosh just a little more into my glass to help me out.

Jeff Davis and Bo started talking about the farm. They asked me all kinds of questions about parasites that the cattle might pick up.

They'd never seemed so interested before, and I found myself launched into a discussion of nematodes and paramecium, methods of pasturing cattle, new vaccines, and other related matters.

All this while the food kept coming. I could put grub away like a sailor, but even I couldn't keep up with the

Hardys. For some reason, I started to try; meanwhile, Billy
Bob kept tipping beer into my glass a splash at a time.

"Better hold off," I told him.

"Come now, Jim, you ain't even had three glasses yet,"
he assured me.

Talk raced on. I'd never noticed how warm and funny
Jeff Davis and Bo could be. They kept me laughing with
their incomparable wits, while the dependable Billy Bob
kept sloshing beer into my glass without letting me have
more than three glasses.

A newcomer entered the oyster bar with a curt nod to the
Hardys. He was tall and blond, and there was a girl with
him.

"There's that Billy Stoner," Bo growled.

"Who's he?" I asked.

"Dang showoff who won ten dollars off me las' week.
'Cause I was drunk!" he bellowed. He stood up. "But I ain't
drunk now!"

"No, you ain't drunk now, Bo," Jeff Davis agreed.

"No, you ain't," I agreed, "I mean, am not."

"Hey, Billy Stoner," Bo called.

"Now, Bo," I began, "let's look at this like sober men."

"Like super men," Jeff intoned, nodding.

Super men sounded much better than sober men, so
much better that I wished I'd thought of it. While I mused
on this, Bo yelled, "You took my ten dollars in a' arm
wrestlin' match last week. Well, I was drunk!"

Billy Stoner walked up to Bo during this speech, but Bo
seemed to forget how to lower his voice. He continued to
yell even with Billy Stoner standing six inches away. "I
want a rematch, is what I say. You lay on 'nother ten and
I'll beat you this time, while I'm sober."

"Super," I corrected.

Billy Stoner's voice, on the other hand, was so quiet that
I couldn't hear him at all.

"What's he sayin'?" I asked Billy Bob.

"He's agreein'," Billy Bob told me.

Billy Stoner and Bo cleaned the condiments off a nearby table and sat down on either side of it, their shirt sleeves rolled up to reveal corded forearms and bulging biceps.

I leaped up, somewhat daunted by not being able to feel my feet on the floor.

"Hold on!" I yelled. "I'll lay on another twenty, Billy Stoner. 'Cause Bo Hardy can beat any man this side of the river at anything."

Stoner gave me a curt nod of agreement and Bo glanced up with an approving look.

"Jim, you're a man!" Jeff Davis said with a slap on my shoulder. "Standin' up for mah brother that way!"

"Jefferson Davis, it's the least a man could do for those cowboy hats you wear in honor of these occasions," I began. Billy Bob clapped his hand over my mouth.

"They're startin'," he said.

Each young man pushed at the other's arm. Billy Stoner stayed cool and calm like ice, but Bo grunted, strained, and got red in the face. The contrast of that extreme passion on the one side against the rigid cynicism on the other moved me very much. It seemed as though somebody should compose a song about it. Instantly I came to understand and love the country western music I had despised so much before. Those singers sang about just such moments as these—the stuff that life was made of.

"Bo, I know you can beat him!" I yelled. "Keep at it!" He looked so noble, so free, so American in his sport shirt, jeans, and hat that I was really overcome with his kindness in befriending me.

By now a considerable knot of people was tangled around the contestants. Cheers were going for both sides.

Billy Stoner at last evidenced sweat on his face and a certain tight-lipped intensity. But it looked as though he was going to win. He forced Bo's hand down toward the table top.

Suddenly Billy Bob barked, "I'll tan your stupid nincom-poop hide if you lose agin, you dung head!"

Bo's eyes popped open, and his passion resumed. The hands came upright again.

"You better be more afeared of me than of him, young man!" Billy Bob roared. "Now you nail him once and fer all and be done with it!"

With one last grunt that became a yell, Bo slammed Billy Stoner's hand to the table. Jeff Davis and I whooped and embraced each other. The room erupted into cheers and congratulations.

"I knew I could do it when I was sober!" Bo said.

"I feel like I could eat again!" Billy Bob said. "Let's have another go 'round."

The contest had filled me with euphoria. I heartily fell to on more oysters and other seafood while Billy Bob supplied me with moderate amounts of beer. I felt, at last, the secure happiness of being with friends. I promised myself that this was a night to remember.

I don't know just when the euphoria wore off. It went by degrees—moments of nausea that were replaced by shorter periods of satisfaction. At last the nausea become perva-sive, then dominant. I wondered what time it could be. The oyster bar was still crowded, and the cigarette smoke seemed suffocating.

"I would like to leave," I declared.

Billy Bob looked at his two brothers, and they nodded.

I stumbled outside while they paid. Anything to get out into the air. But it was a disappointment. The air was too warm to be refreshing.

The Hardy brothers came out and helped me to the truck. I sat on the end by the door, and in my deepening misery I thought I couldn't feel worse.

But then Billy Bob began to rev the engine. "Fresh air will do you good," he said. He turned on the vent full force.

The blast of desert-hot air that hit my face prompted an immediate response. I threw up all over my lap.

Jeff got the window down while Billy Bob peeled out with a roar of seared rubber.

"We've got to git you cleaned up, Jim," Jeff said. He and Bo used their hands to scrape the muck off me and throw it out the window. Even in my distress, I marvelled at their rock-hard sensibilities.

The worst happened several times more as we sped and jolted back across the Savannah. But each time, Jeff Davis got me by the hair and directed my head out the open window. Of course his hands were soiled with it, and hence my hair received enough of the substance to make me smell from head to foot like the inside of a shark's stomach.

I was wishing mightily that I would pass out. Somewhere along the way, my wish must have been granted.

It was a good deal later when I came around, feeling what I had wanted for what seemed like hours—cool air. I was slung by the arms between Billy Bob and Bo. They were marching me—or trying to march me—down a path through the woods.

"Where's Jeff?" I asked.

"Down at the truck," Billy Bob grunted. "He started t' feel poorly hisself."

My heart was wrung for him. "We can't just leave him behind," I said, though I had no idea where we were going.

"We'll walk him next," Billy Bob promised. "First, we got to get you on your feet."

"I think I would like to go home," I began.

"No, boy, you'd get the bed spins then," Billy Bob told me.

"Everything's spinning anyway," I said.

Suddenly Bo gave a yell. My head rang from it. "Look out, Billy Bob! It's the ghost!"

"Durn my hide, yes! Let's go, Jim! It's real!"

Both men slipped out from under my arms.

"Come on, Jim! Run!"

I hit the ground on my face and rolled over onto my back. Blood spurted from my nose and down my chin.

Yes, it was the squaw, standing in front of the white deer. She seemed awfully big and terrible, but she came closer as though a little hesitant.

I hardly noticed the deer at all, but I stared hard at the squaw, wondering just what she thought about living mortals.

"How," I said at last.

The cool breeze blew her hair back a little. Her braids caught the wind and fanned out slightly. I couldn't make out her face very well, but after all, she was a ghost. Not transparent, but obscure.

Next thing I knew, I was stumbling back up the trail. I found the truck more by accident than by design.

"Jim, Jim!" Billy Bob grabbed me. "You all right? We thought you was right behind us."

"You'd better take me home," I said.

"Coffee'll fix y'up. Come on." He helped me into the truck. Bo sat right next to me, and he and Billy Bob managed to lever Jeff in on the other side. He sat between them, his head on his knees.

"Looks like you've banged your face up," Bo said to me.

The truck stopped, and Billy Bob helped Jefferson Davis up to the house while Bo took charge of me.

"Just take me home," I said.

"Jim, we can't leave you 'lone in this state, boy. Come in jus' t' get yer face washed and some coffee in ya," he said.

He dragged me up the porch and through the front door.

"Pee-yew! What in tarnation have you boys got into?" Lem Hardy's voice asked. The living room lights seemed much too bright. I squinted and wondered what was going on. Why was Lem still up?

"You're back early," Lem was saying, and then I heard footsteps that somehow I recognized, and Anne's gasp. "Is that Jim?"

"Yeah, he's had a little too much, I b'lieve. Say hi to the lady, college boy," Billy Bob said, holding my face up by the chin.

Anne's face swam into view, and somehow I realized what I looked and smelled like. The sudden understanding knocked me sober for a moment.

10 - Hung Over

"Jack, I need help."

"I'll be right there."

I fell asleep from the time I let the receiver fall until I heard Jack's steps on the stairs outside my rooms. The door was unlocked, and he let himself in.

"You all right, Jim?" he asked.

"No."

"You want the treatment?"

"Yes. Whatever it takes."

He hung up the receiver for me and went into the bathroom. I heard the shower start pounding out water at full force.

Jack went into the kitchenette. I heard him put coffee on. He also put the tea kettle on. He came back and threw my soiled clothing into a pile in the corner and opened a window.

At last he got me up and half carried me into the bathroom, which, by the way, was about the size of a big phone booth. Without a word, he pushed me into the shower.

Freezing cold water bombarded me. I yelled and would have jumped out, but he pushed me back in.

"You said you wanted the treatment. This what it takes."

He grabbed a washcloth and scrubbed it vigorously

across my forehead. After about a hundred scrubs, he scrubbed it over the top of my head, and then up the back of my head. It felt like heaven when he stopped.

"Come out," he said. He toweled off my head as though it were a shoe he was buffing.

While I toweled off the rest of me, he went into the kitchenette and returned with the Alka-Seltzer. I took it without complaint. At last, as I dragged on a t-shirt and some cut-offs, he reappeared with the coffee.

"You might want tea instead."

"No, coffee," I said.

I had no living room, only two hard-backed chairs and a small table over by the room's only window. After slipping on my sunglasses, I opened the curtains. A warm block of sunlight fell across us. It felt good.

I sipped the coffee, and when it was finished asked for another cup. Jack brought it to me.

"I made a jackass out of myself last night," I said.

"Drink too much?"

"Way too much, Jack. I can't talk about all of it, but I've got to tell you what they did to me." My voice shook on that last part, and Jack's surprise showed on his face.

"What do you mean, Jim?"

"They made me look a fool to Anne, Jack. They set me up. They did it on purpose."

"Whoa, steady. Tell me what you remember."

I told him. I had to omit details about the food, and I didn't bother with a long account of the arm-wrestling match. But I told him about the squaw and, finally, about being dragged before Anne.

"Covered with all that?" Jack asked as he nodded at the pile of clothes.

I gave a slow nod of my head. "Blood, mud, and vomit," I said. My throat got tight. "Why, Jack? I see that they must know I love her. But why would they do that to me?"

"Who'd ha' thought they could be so vicious?" he asked.

"I'm an outsider to them," I said. "They must resent me for wanting to take her away."

"I don't know, boy. It was ugly of them. 'Course," he added with a glance at me, "they didn't pour that beer down your throat."

"Don't think I haven't kicked myself about it over and over, Jack. I woke up here, and it was the first thing I thought of. I kept dozing and waking up, and each time it was to that. I ruined myself."

"I won't mention it again," he promised, "and you know, if Anne's the gal I think she is, she'll know you're 'shamed. She won't say nothin'. Not to you nor anyone else."

"I'll apologize to her," I said. "I think better of her than to be drunk like that in front of her."

He took out a cigarette and lit it. "What a bunch of cusses," he said. "An' after all you done for 'em, free of charge, out on that farm."

On Sunday nights at church, Anne came without the rest of her family. That next Sunday night, I stopped her as she was on her way to choir rehearsal.

"Anne," I said, and I felt my face burn before I could say anything else, "I wondered if I could speak to you a second."

"Certainly," she said, but she looked wary and even a little pained. I supposed that she was embarrassed.

"Well, Anne," I told her, "I . . . I know that, ah . . . well, I don't think it was polite of me. I mean, I think highly of you, Anne."

"Thank you," she said.

"So highly that I'm ashamed of what I did Friday night," I blurted. "I can't undo it, but I wish—if it has to be one of my mistakes—that it hadn't been paraded in front of you. I really am sorry."

"Jim, are you sorry that you got drunk or sorry that I saw you?" she asked gently.

"Both," I told her. "But I never would have realized the first if I hadn't experienced the second. Neither will ever happen again."

"Well, it's all right then," she said. She started to walk away, and I said after her, "I hope that someday I win back your respect, Anne. I hope you'll give me another chance."

She actually stopped, turned around, and came back. "Jim, I see that your feelings are hurt. I'm sorry," she said.

"Sorry?" I asked.

"I don't think that it was all your fault." She put her hand on my sleeve and seemed ready to say more, but then she changed her mind. She seemed even more embarrassed and pained, and I realized that she had to know that her brothers had planned the whole thing. She must at least have guessed that I was in love with her, and that they were thwarting me.

"Let's just go on as before," she said.

"Thank you, Anne."

But we were both blushing and uncomfortable. We hurriedly separated, and I spent the rest of the evening feeling almost as wretched as I had felt on Saturday morning.

11 - Anne's News

Aiken County is known for its thoroughbred horses. Jack kept some supplies in stock for the horse breeders, including combs and brushes, but most of their gear they purchased from specialty stores.

On Tuesday morning Anne came into the store, all breathless and excited about something.

"H'lo, Anne," Jack said guardedly. At the moment he didn't trust any of the Hardys.

"Hello, Jack. Oh, Jim," she called, looking right past him to me, "you'll never guess what! A llama breeder from Ohio is coming this weekend."

"That's terrific, Anne," I said. I would have felt restrained in front of her, but it was so obvious that her mind was all on her news that I didn't need to.

"Is this a business trip," I asked, "or does he just need a stopover place?"

"A little of both," she told me. "He and his wife have been so kind to me, Jim. Their name is Mayehuus. And he's thinking of buying Snow Queen."

"But she's your favorite."

"Well, I know, and I had decided that the herd was too small for me to do any selling yet. But he mentioned such a good price for her, Jim. That is, if he decides to take her."

"I thought solid whites like Snowy didn't sell so well," I said.

"Mr. Mayehuus says that tastes will differ as the market

grows. And Snowy's got such good conformation. Her legs, back, and ears are perfect. She's got reasonably good wool, too."

Anne glanced around the store. "I wanted to go to work right away on grooming all of them, and I actually snapped the handle of my slicker brush. Do you have any?"

"I think so. Let's go see." I gave Jack a broad grin as I passed him. At last things were going my way.

I found the brush for her. As I rang it up, I said, "Now, Anne, if there's anything you need, please call me, even if you have to call me at home. I'd really like this to come off for you."

"Thank you, Jim. I want everything to go well with him. I'm cleaning up the whole place, and I've even brought some of Mother's quilts down to dry-clean and put on the guest bed."

"How's the . . . uh . . . Barn Cat doing?" I asked.

She shook her head. "I haven't seen him. His paw could become gangrenous, couldn't it?"

"Yes, if the band on it is tight enough."

"If I see him I'll call right away. Maybe I could entice him into a box trap for you."

"That's an idea." I handed the bag to her. "Good luck, Anne." She offered me one bright, sweet smile, nodded goodbye to Jack, and hurried out. Her frank enthusiasm and eagerness had made our awkwardness a thing of the past, and I stood for a moment looking after her, wishing that somehow I could always be a part of Anne's happiness.

"Well now, wasn't that sweet!" Jack taunted as the door closed behind her.

"Come on, Jack."

"Looks t' me like yer doin' fine in her good graces," he observed.

"Well, I talked to her Sunday night. And besides," I told him, "she's on cloud nine about that buyer. I hope it goes well. She could do with having her name passed around among the bigger llama breeders."

Anne wasn't the only Hardy to come into the store that day. I had avoided Billy Bob, Bo, and Jefferson Davis, but it hadn't occurred to me that they might come to the store.

About noontime, Billy Bob came in. There were several customers browsing, and I was just going to the back room to restock. Billy Bob ignored me as he stepped up to the counter. "Hey, Jack, you got any—"

"No!" Jack snapped.

"What if—"

"No," Jack said again. He didn't raise his voice, but his tone drew every eye.

"Look, Jack—," Billy Bob began again.

Jack slapped his hand down on the counter top. "We ain't got what you want, Billy Bob. We ain't got it," he said.

Billy Bob just stared at him. I was frozen at the back door. The part-time boy at the counter stared at Jack. All of the other chatter in the store stopped.

Billy Bob pushed back his cap and tried to stand on his dignity. He hesitated, swallowed, and said, "My pa's been a customer here for twenty years."

"Your pa's a customer in good standing," Jack affirmed. "But you ain't. Now I think it's time you left."

Billy Bob slapped his cap against his leg and strode out, his face flushed.

Later, as I cleaned up my lunch things so that Jack could eat, Jack came in without even a word of what had passed earlier.

"Jack," I said.

"Hmm."

"Well," I began. He looked blank. "I guess I thought I didn't have any friends here," I told him. "I was wrong."

"You got plenty o' friends, young man," he said brusquely. "The Hardys ain't everybody." He pulled his sandwich and cake out of his lunch bag and tossed them onto the table.

"Thanks all the same."

"You're welcome."

12 - Anne Has a Bad Day

The jangle of the phone crashed into my dreams.

I groped for the receiver in my sleep, knocked the alarm clock off the narrow end table, and at last found my target.

"Hello!"

Anne's voice instantly brought me up from my waves of sleep. She sounded tearful and frightened.

"Oh, Jim, it's Anne. Snow Queen's limping, and the buyer arrived last night. Can you come?"

"I'll be right there, Anne."

I fumbled into my clothes while my mind tried to formulate guesses as to why a healthy female llama should develop a limp. I made a list in my head of questions to ask Anne about Snowy's diet, recent exercise, and nail trimming.

I was scheduled to work at ten and had planned on sleeping until nine. But at six, Horse Creek Valley glowed under ribbons of pink, orange, gray, and gold; fingers of mist lingered in the low places. I was glad that I hadn't slept through it. It was a glorious Saturday morning.

Anne met me out on the driveway. Her hair was down and streaming behind her, looking almost blond in the glare of the headlights.

Night shadows still lingered on the Hardy farm, which

lay on low ground. I leaped out of the car, jammed a few items into my pockets, and hurried with her out to the "goat" pasture.

"She was just fine yesterday," Anne said as we went, "but this morning when I brought grain to them, she was favoring her back left leg very badly. Oh, Jim, you don't think a snake bit her, do you?"

"No, I don't think so," I told her. "A poisonous snake bite would cause immediate swelling. Where is she?"

"Just down this rise by the far fence line," Anne told me.

We hurried down to the far side of the pasture. Snow Queen looked peaceful enough as she lay, neck and head up, ears alert, and watched us approach.

But she resisted getting up. Anne tugged on the halter and urged her, but it wasn't until I suddenly ran at her that she arose. She gave me a disdainful glance as I examined her haunch and leg.

I had at first guessed that Snowy was suffering lameness from an unaccustomed overexertion, but I had guessed prematurely. My fingers encountered matted wool, and in the imperfect light I couldn't be sure, but I thought there was coagulated blood spattered in small patches here and there.

My probing became more gentle, and I found several very small wounds. "Let's get her to higher ground," I told Anne. "I need more light."

We walked her up to the highest ground in the goat pasture, where the light was much better. I could see from her gait that Snow Queen was not badly hurt.

I had my small forceps and clippers, and I went to work clearing away the wool, which was, indeed, spattered with blood.

"She's got buckshot in her thigh," I told Anne. As quickly as I could, I removed five pellets. I rechecked to make sure I hadn't missed any and then straightened up.

Anne was stunned. "Who would have shot Snow Queen?" she asked.

"Well, whoever did, missed," I told her. "In fact, these five may have been ricochets or may have been fired from a distance. They didn't lodge very deep."

We were interrupted by a "Halloo!" across the field. We looked up to see a cheery, round little man in a fishing cap wave to us.

"Oh, dear," Anne said, "that's Mr. Mayehuus, and his llama's been shot!"

"Anything wrong?" Mr. Mayehuus called as he walked toward us.

Anne was tongue-tied, so I called back, "Oh, not very much." I gently pulled Anne's hand off Snow Queen's halter. The llama walked away and lay down again.

"Tell him after breakfast," I whispered to her, "after a really good breakfast."

"Oh!" she said, reminded of something. "Would you like to stay to breakfast?"

It was only polite to ask me after I'd come out on such short notice so early, but I shook my head. "How could I explain myself to him?"

"Ah! Mr. Mayehuus!" I exclaimed as he came up too close for us to whisper. I held out my hand, shook his, and introduced myself.

"Just out to look over the llamas," I said. "Beautiful animals, aren't they? I hear that you raise them, too."

Mr. Mayehuus was too jolly and friendly a soul to resist the bait I threw. "Well, yes, they're a hobby of mine," he said. "I've picked up a few here and there—about sixty now."

"What a life you must lead," I told him. "Anne's small herd is enough to keep us laughing. Sixty must be quite a show from dawn to dusk."

"Well, as you know, they're a regal animal, too," he added.

He fell into step with me as I walked to the barn to wash my hands at the outside faucet. I squatted down and washed off, and just then I spied a small, furry bundle huddled into a crevice between the floor boards.

"Shhh," I breathed to Mr. Mayehuus.

"What?" he whispered.

"There's the cat!"

Anne was approaching, and I waved her back.

I rose slowly and carefully crept up into the barn, easing myself across the worn and splintered boards that might creak at any moment.

I realized that the cat had wormed its way into a pretty snug niche. All I was seeing was the top of the rump and the fluffy tail. I'd likely get scratched when I pulled it out, but this time I wouldn't let go.

I leaned closer until at last I was right over it. The llamas, curious over the three humans clustered around the barn door, gathered around. Crackers went straight for Mr. Mayehuus, clipped him on the back of the head with her jaw, and accidentally knocked him down with her neck and chest.

He yelled.

The black form at my feet started. I grabbed it before it could dart away and pulled it out of the floorboards.

The barn seemed to explode. Something like liquid fire in aerosol form threw me blindly back across the prostrate Mr. Mayehuus. I fell and landed on my back.

Llamas exploded out of the barn, leaping right over us. Anne screamed. I scrubbed my sleeve across my face and eyes while fumbling to roll off Mr. Mayehuus. But in spite of his age and bulk, he scrambled out first and quickly doused his head under the faucet.

"A skunk!" Anne sobbed. "Oh, Jim, all the llamas. Mr. Mayehuus, I'm sorry!"

Mayehuus grabbed me by the jacket collar and unselfishly pulled me into the flow of water.

"Not at all," I heard him say before the water thundered into my ears.

13 - Skunked

"Jack, I need help."

"I thought you'd given that up!"

"A skunk got me, Jack."

"I'll be right there."

It took him about a half hour, and he staggered in under two grocery bags full of canned tomato juice.

I stuck my head out of the shower and nodded at him when he came in.

"What'd you do with your clothes?" he yelled over the sound of the pounding water.

"Put them in a Hefty and threw them out the window."

"Turn off that water, and let's try this."

He doused me with tomato juice. I couldn't decide if it was working or not. We tried it three times, rinsing off with water in between. Then he brought out the large economy-size baking soda boxes.

At last there was nothing left to try. After I dried off and got into clean clothes, I did feel that, yes, the treatment had reduced the smell a good deal. I certainly would be constantly reminded that I'd grabbed a skunk, but if I kept my distance nobody else would know.

"You get yourself into the durn'dest situations, Jim," Jack told me. "Now where you been?"

"Hardys' farm," I told him. "I thought I'd grabbed their barn cat, but I hadn't."

"Honestly, boy, that place is bad luck for you."

"Well, it was Anne's bad luck today," I said. "That buyer is there, and all three of us got sprayed by the skunk."

He shook his head and glanced at his watch. "Ain't hardly eight yet. I'll make us some breakfast."

My small kitchenette was more like a walk-in closet than anything else. I sat at the table and talked to Jack while he cooked. He'd brought along a dozen eggs and some sausage—dietary staples in Horse Creek Valley. I wasn't insensitive to Jack's generosity. Every time I needed him, he came through for me.

I had respected his generosity in dealing with people and had marvelled at the crusty exterior that hid such a kind heart. But it wasn't until that scene with Billy Bob that I realized that Jack was my friend. He had fooled me all along. Unlike my hero, Wagner Nesbitt, I couldn't see through crusty exteriors. It had taken me all these months to realize that Jack was patroning me through my initiation into Horse Creek Valley.

He brought two plates of sausage and eggs to the table and sat down.

Even though my sudden understanding of Jack brought a lump to my throat, there wasn't any point in saying anything. Jack barked at sentimentality.

As we ate, he said, "One thing 'bout you, Jim, you keep me innerested in what c'n happen next."

I glanced at him and tried to grin, but it kind of hurt.

"Y'sure you want to go as a vet full time?" he asked.

"Sure, I'm sure!"

"Because," he added, "I don't know that Horse Creek Valley's ever goin' t' need a full-time vet. And you know, Augusta and Aiken 're crammed full of 'em."

I nodded on that.

"Now that I'm fifty-ish," he added, "when I see a spring mornin' like this, I kind of feel it, y'know?"

"Feel what?" I asked.

"That I'm fifty-ish, boy! Ain't you payin' attention? Anyway," he added, "it's time for me t' get out more. Enjoy myself—go fishin', go huntin', do more of what I've always wanted to do."

I nodded. I was already working full time for him, but I wondered if he was hinting that I should become manager.

"How'd you like to buy half of the store from me?" he asked. I nearly choked.

"Become part owner?" I gasped.

"Partner," he said. "Junior partner for a year, but then full partner."

"Jack, I don't know what to say."

"Well, think on it a while," he told me. "But not too long, 'cause I'd like t' get some of this burden offa me."

I was too thunderstruck to say much for the rest of the meal. Buying in to the store would be the chance of a lifetime, but it would mean devoting myself to it full time. And yet, to own a business, or even part of one, meant security. And there could never be a partner to equal Jack. I already knew that he was fair, honest, and generous.

He chatted about other things, as carelessly as though he'd offered to sell me half his fishing rod. I was still too dazed to answer, until he said, "Why, I near forgot to tell you. Howie Dugan saw the ghost last night."

"I thought Howie saw it a lot," I said.

"Yeah, but last night he shot at it."

"He what?"

"I told him it was a dang fool thing t' do!" Jack exclaimed, nodding. "It's just someone dressed up like a squaw, an' he coulda kilt—"

I jumped up.

"What's wrong?" Jack asked.

"Jack, what happened when he shot it?" I asked.

"Oh, nuthin'. He told me he missed it—just shot up the dirt around her feet and watched both squaw and doe run like wild horses outta there. He was drunk when he done it, I reckon." Jack squinted up at me. "You ain't finished your eggs, boy."

"I've got to go! I'll see you at the store!"

I ran out the door and down the steps, hopped into my car, and raced for the Hardy farm.

14 - The Avenging Vet

I pulled up at the Hardy farm in time to see Jefferson Davis saunter into their old machine shed.

"Jefferson Davis!" I yelled. I jumped out of the car. "Jefferson Davis!" I didn't know if he heard me or not. I ran across the grass to the machine shed.

He met me at the doorway. I didn't challenge him; I didn't say a word. But he saw it coming and put up his arms to block me as I lunged at him.

I belted him across the face, and I hardly felt it when his fist whacked my ear. My blow drove him back into the shed. He threw himself at me as I came in, and I punched him again with so much force that my first two knuckles split against his chin. He staggered from it, and I hit him with a left hook.

Jefferson Davis obviously preferred wrestling, but boxing was all I knew. I'd had a year of it in high school. He was still game enough to try to grapple with me. He lunged again. I missed with the right, but the left connected.

Now that it came down to it, all that I could remember from high school boxing was the straight right, left hook combination. I knew that sooner or later he had to get around it.

He did, and he threw me to the ground in a bearlike hold. But my first punches had stunned him. I worked my right hand free and punched the side of his head until I felt him change his grip to get a better one. I drove my knee into his stomach with enough force to make him fall away, and then I was on top, punching for all I was worth.

I might as well admit that in a cool temper I would never have consented to a fight with any of the Hardy brothers. But it was something of a pleasant surprise to realize that I was more than holding my own against Jefferson Davis.

I dragged him up by his shirt.

"Billy Bob!" he bawled. "Bo!"

Without thinking, I dropped him and ran to the sliding wooden doors. Only one was open. I closed it. He jumped on me from behind to stop me, but we both knew he was about licked. He sank his teeth into my back, and more from instinct than anger, I swung around to get him off and punched his nose so hard that blood spurted out. He fell back to the dirt floor. I set the bar in place across the doors.

I pulled Jeff Davis's head up by the hair.

"What d'ya want, anyway?" he asked. "It was Billy Bob's idea to take you. I—"

"Shut up!" I said. "This isn't about that!" I hauled him up by his underarms and set his back against the wall. "You nearly got Snow Queen killed last night." I thumped him against the wall.

"She was just nicked, Vet."

I shook him again. "You could have ruined her for sale! You know that!"

He looked around as though searching for an excuse, but then he said, "Yeah, okay. It was close."

"Why are you playing with Anne's dreams?" I asked him. I thumped him into the wall again. "The llamas are hers! Selling that llama meant everything to her!"

"Okay, okay!" he said. "I won't go out no more!"

"It's not okay!" I yelled. I threw him down. He just lay there and looked up at me. "You three treat Anne like she's your personal property," I said. "As long as you have a good time, that's all that matters!"

"What do you know about us?" he asked.

"More than I can stand, I'll tell you that!" I said. "You're not going to destroy this dream of Anne's, Jeff Davis. Don't you or your brothers ever touch those llamas again. They're hers!"

"It ain't your business," he said.

"And you're going to go to her and tell her that you've been playing the squaw with Snow Queen as the deer," I added, "or I'll tell her. And I'll tell her that's how Snow Queen picked up the buckshot."

He scrambled up on shaky legs. "Vet, she'll cry," he said.

"I'd cry, too," I told him, "if I were Anne and had brothers like you three."

"But what good will it do?" he asked.

"If anything can, Jeff, it will make you responsible," I told him. "You aren't going to pull tricks like this on her. Not while I'm around. I won't let you."

This last part came out unadvisedly. I realized it was a mistake as soon as I heard myself say it. But I affected nonchalance as I pulled down the bar and opened the door.

"You act like you're in love with her or something," he said in a tone unmistakably mocking.

I didn't know why he would mock this idea, but I wouldn't deny it to anyone. "I am in love with her," I said. His jaw dropped open, and I strode away.

I would just make it to work on time, and I knew I'd be a sight to see. I wondered if even Jack's crustiness would give way to shock at seeing me in my present condition.

On the way down to my car I passed Billy Bob's parked truck. I reached in through the open window, pulled open the glove compartment, and plucked out the black wig that Jeff Davis had used. The disappearance of the wig would at least slow him down from any encore performances he planned on making.

It was five until ten when I walked into the feed store. Though the store opened at eight on most mornings, things were slow just then.

Jack's eyes widened when I walked in, but all he said was, "I wonder if you feel like tellin' me why you left such a good breakfast behind, young man. All for what looks like a fight."

I walked past him to go to the back. "I beat up Jefferson Davis Hardy," I said.

"What for?" he asked as the door swung closed behind me.

I opened the door and said, "Because he's the squaw, and he was using one of Anne's llamas for the doe."

I went into the back room. It was too much for Jack. He came after me. The door closed behind him.

"Are you sure?" he asked. "How do you know?"

"The wig's out in my car," I told him. "I took it out of Billy Bob's truck."

Jack studied me a moment and leaned against the wall.

"Now, Jim," he said, as he lit a cigarette with a look of great enjoyment, "I'm the man what's helped you when you was broke, when you was sick, and when you'd been skunked." He exhaled with that same look of pleasure. "I know you'll tell old Jack the whole story o' how you solved this case and beat up Jefferson Davis Hardy."

We both laughed, and I told him.

"I should have guessed something was up that night that I first saw the squaw," I admitted. "I was on my way to the Hardy farm and saw it, and an hour or so later, when the boys came in, Jeff Davis went right into the bathroom without coming into the kitchen. He must have been in costume."

Jack nodded. I continued.

"And then the night they got me drunk, Jeff Davis play-acted that he was sick. Bo and Billy Bob walked me up into the woods, and then I saw the squaw. We weren't far from the Hardy farm. Jeff had time to get the llama and get back while they walked me around in circles.

"Afterward I imagine they left the llama tied up while they took me to the farm. But in the truck Bo stayed between me and Jeff. I guess Jeff still had makeup on. He likely stuffed the wig into the glove compartment."

Jack looked thoughtful.

"What tipped me off was when you told me Howie had shot at the ghosts," I said. "I went to the Hardy farm this morning to pull buckshot out of Snow Queen's flank. As soon as you told me, I knew that the three boys were in on the ghost, but it clicked all of a sudden that Jeff Davis was actually playing the squaw."

"So you whupped him good," Jack added.

"Yes," I told him, "I think it was one of the best ten minutes of my life!"

Jack couldn't suppress a grin.

"Think he'll tell Anne you fought him?"

"He'll have to. He's got to apologize to Anne," I told Jack. "If he doesn't, I plan to tell her myself about him and the squaw."

"You tryin' to teach him a lesson?" Jack asked. "Well, maybe you'll get through, but I doubt it."

"And I told him that I love her," I added.

"Uh oh." Jack stopped in the act of lighting another cigarette and looked at me.

15 - The Hardys Make a Request

On Sunday morning at church, the Hardys sat in their same order in the pew. Jeff Davis had some swelling and discoloration around one eye, but his nose was almost back to normal.

I still had tape on my knuckles. My thoughts throughout the first hymn and the prayer were anything but fit for church or Sunday morning. The exultation of having beaten him roared through me all over again.

Billy Bob actually shot a glance back at me, and I met his eye with a cool and determined look of my own. Startled to find me watching him, he turned back around.

Anne glanced over at him and then back at me, her expression unreadable but not hostile in any way.

After the service, they filed past me. Billy Bob actually said, "H'lo, Jim," in a sheepish, half-hearted way. I nodded at him. Jeff Davis went by with his head down, and Bo gave me a look of both amusement and incomprehension. Anne looked up at me.

"I hope things turned out well with the buyer," I said.

Her eyes became wet, but she blinked and said, "We'll see. He's thinking it over." She looked almost ready to say something else, but then she walked away.

Lem slapped my shoulder, nodded, and went on.

But that night when Anne came to church alone, I risked approaching her.

"I told Jefferson Davis that I would talk to you if he didn't," I said.

"He told me," she said. She didn't seem to know what to say, so I added, "Anne, I made him tell you because I'm afraid that the llamas would be used in other jokes. I know that they're valuable. And I don't want games to be played with them."

Her eyes shone with tears again. "Well," she said, and her voice shook, "I was very upset."

"So was I," I told her.

"I just wish that what I did wasn't a game to them!" she exclaimed. She nearly started to cry in earnest. But she controlled herself. She couldn't look up, but she added, "The llamas are goats to them. Snow Queen was nothing but a part in one of their jokes. That barn where the skunk hid—it's the most run down on the farm."

There wasn't anything to say that wouldn't make her feel worse. I felt—probably much more strongly than Anne did—that she was outnumbered and unappreciated at home.

I changed the subject. "What did the buyer say?"

She couldn't resist a smile. "He took it pretty well. He even laughed about the skunk, later. But when I told him about Snow Queen, he wanted to be certain that she's in good health and would be able to stand the stress of a move."

"You still have her, then?" I asked.

"Yes. He wants you to certify that she can travel."

"But he does want to buy her?"

"Oh, yes. He'll give me the price he quoted, and he said that if I bring her up I can bring up Gerda, too, and he'll have his stud Buckeye breed her."

"That's terrific!"

"Except that I don't have a way to get them up there," she

told me. "But Jefferson Davis says he'll find me a van."

I nodded, and she smiled. "Jeff Davis really is sorry," she said. "I'm afraid that I lost my temper when he confessed to me. And then I cried. None of them like it when I cry. They don't know what to do. They feel so guilty."

"Maybe you should cry more," I told her.

She lifted her chin. "I don't think so," she said. I smiled at her.

"Well, Anne," I told her, "if I can help, please call on me. How many of you will drive up to Ohio?"

"Oh, just me," she said. "I'd better get to choir."

I didn't like the idea of Anne driving six hundred miles without help. Apparently, I wasn't alone in that opinion. The next morning when I pulled up to work, the three Hardy brothers were lounging against the front of the store.

I wasn't sure what they wanted, and Jack hadn't come yet. But I was too proud to behave as though intimidated. So I switched off the engine, got out of the car, and walked up to them.

"Can I help you?" I asked.

"Now, Jim," Billy Bob said, "we ain't come to fight."

"Whatever you've come for, just say it, or do it, and leave," I said.

Jeff Davis tipped up his cap. "We come to 'pologize," he said.

"Okay."

"And t' ask you a favor," Billy Bob added.

"What could you want from me?"

"It's for Anne," he told me.

"For Anne?"

"You're in love with her, ain't you?" Jeff Davis asked. My face burned and I stepped up toward him. He wasn't going to throw that in my face. It wasn't a joke.

"Whoa, Jim!" Billy Bob exclaimed. "He's just askin'. Did you really say that?"

"Yes," I said. I looked at Jeff Davis. "Did you tell Anne I said it?"

"No," Jeff Davis replied.

"No," Billy Bob agreed, and Bo shook his head.

"We just thought maybe you'd help her out, then," Billy Bob said.

"Of course I would help her out," I said. "But it's not your business."

"Well, she won't ask you, so we thought we would," he told me.

"What do you want, then?"

"She's set to go to Ohio next weekend," he said. "Drive up Friday night and drive back Saturday night. We c'n only git the van that long."

"Can't you go up with her?"

He solemnly shook his head. "She don't want our help, Jim."

"She don't?" I echoed. "Doesn't?" I corrected.

"She's mad at us," Jeff Davis said. "On account of the squaw. She says she don't need our help."

"Anne's got a lot of courage," I said. "And pride."

"Yeah, and the skull of a mule," Billy Bob added. "She don't want us along, and she acted like she was doing Jefferson Davis a big favor by lettin' him borrow a van for her."

"I'll offer to go with her," I told them.

They all nodded and sauntered back to the truck.

16 - Surprising Discoveries

Jefferson Davis did a lot of work on the van before he turned it over to us. He unbolted the seats and laid down heavy matting and carpet, which he secured with duct tape. He and the other two brothers gave the engine a thorough tune-up.

They had just finished when I pulled up on Friday evening. Even though I had worked all day, I felt fresh and eager to go. With Snow Queen on a lead, Anne came up to the van, which was parked on a hill to create a slight ramp effect. After only a little coaxing, the white llama walked up easily and leaped into the van with no sign of stiffness or pain. Billy Bob stood by with Gerda on a lead. Gerda was eighteen months old, what I call a tri-color. Her dominant color was brown, and she had roan and black markings. While Snow Queen was regal, high-strung, and yet gracious, Gerda was more compact, jovial in her bearing, and unabashedly curious. Animal Crackers had taught Gerda some of her own odd habits, and so Gerda was less shy of people than most llamas. She expected treats from them and usually got some.

Anne took the lead and led Gerda up, and the young llama nimbly hopped inside.

"Ready?" I asked her. She smiled at me, that same type

of smile I'd seen before, but reserved for her father. Lem came out to see us off, and Anne kissed him goodbye.

"Bye, Sissy," Billy Bob said as she walked past him.

"Goodbye. Are you ready, Jim?"

"All ready. See ya, men," I called. I waved cheerily to them as Anne pulled out.

One thing that Jefferson Davis might have put up in the van was a screen to separate humans and llamas. They were good travelers, but from the start they decided that looking out the front windshield was the best way to travel. And not only did they want to look out the windshield, they breathed down our necks. Noses working and wrinkling, they strained their faces forward.

"This could get difficult," I said.

"Oh, they'll settle down," Anne laughed as she guided the van onto the highway. "I feel so good about this trip, Jim. I'm so glad you offered to come along."

"Oh, my pleasure. I'd like to get a look at that llama farm," I said.

Gerda leaned down and managed to flip open the picnic basket Anne had brought along.

"Whoa, girl, hands off—I mean, nose out!" I told her, pushing her nose back.

Anne laughed and I laughed. At last the llamas did settle down. They lay down, but they kept their heads up to see the sights.

We took Highway 25 north toward where we would pick up the interstate through the mountains into Tennessee and then through Kentucky. The Mayehuus place wasn't far across the line into Ohio.

I had seldom had Anne all to myself, and at the moment she seemed so sunny, happy, and charming that I was delighted just to look at her and listen to her. I don't remember what she talked about at first, but she charmed me into conversation.

We talked about the farm, my college days, the store, what it had been like up North when I'd grown up, and my own introduction to Horse Creek Valley. I told her all about some of my adventures, and I told her about Didee.

"Do you still go up to see him?" she asked, looking from the road to me and back again.

"I mean to, but I've been busy," I said. "Why?"

"I wish I could meet him, too," she said.

"You'd be welcome to come along, but what would your father say?"

"He wouldn't like it," she said frankly. "But I'd like to go along." She had her chin up again. I smiled at her.

"Fine with me."

She told me more about her family, about her mother, and about her mother's illness.

Daylight waned. We switched off driving, and our talk become more sporadic. Anne had fixed up a basket for us, and we ate sandwiches and coffee as I drove along.

We'd just finished when suddenly Gerda stood up and thrust her face forward over the front seat.

"Hey!" I yelled.

"Oh!" Anne exclaimed.

Suddenly Snow Queen stood up and pushed her face forward.

"Jim, what's wrong with them?" Anne asked.

Eyes quizzical and nose wrinkling, Gerda turned her face into mine and looked me in the eye.

"Gerda, move!" I yelled, and pushed her away.

"Sit down, Snowy! Cush! Cush!" Anne exclaimed. She got up on her knees on the seat and tried to push Snow Queen back. At last both llamas lay back down.

"What did that?" Anne asked.

"I don't know. You're the expert on llamas."

"They're almost immune to carsickness," she said. "Well, they seem all right now."

Anne sat down again, but just as she did, both llamas

stood up again. This time they stayed toward the back of the van, but they would not settle back down.

"Why won't they lie down?" I asked.

We spent the next few minutes shooting nervous glances at the back of the van. Snow Queen hummed. In the cramped confines of the van they stepped forward and thrust their heads into the front.

"Oh, Jim, what could it mean?" Anne asked as she turned around and pushed them back.

They were more insistent this time, but at last they settled down again.

"They don't seem carsick," Anne said. Suddenly she exclaimed, "Jim! I know what's wrong! Pull over! Quick!"

I signaled and was just pulling to the side of the highway when Snow Queen stood up, then Gerda. I heard a noise peculiar to barnyards and I understood Anne's alarm. The noise must have influenced Gerda's ability to "hold it," for she also began to unburden herself. (There are some real disadvantages to animals that follow the herd!)

I pulled to a stop, and we both leaped out. It was dark by now, and in the red glare of our flashing emergency lights, we opened up the van and quickly pulled them out. They finished their business along the side of the inter-state, as far off the road as we could get them.

Passing cars and trucks slowed down and turned on their brights.

"There're paper towels up in the picnic basket and a whisk broom under the seat," Anne said.

I got them and went to work on cleaning out the back of the van. We'd reacted pretty quickly, but not quickly enough. Did I ever wish we had figured out the llama language earlier! Next time we'd know.

We didn't have any regular cleaning supplies. I did the best I could. I took out all the indoor/outdoor carpet that Jeff Davis had put in the van and shook it out vigorously. Then I restuck the duct tape on it to hold it down.

The llamas were willing enough to hop back inside, but as we started again, I drove with the vent on full blast.

Anne was tired, and I told her, "Better get some sleep. I may need you to take over again in a few hours."

She nodded and rested her head on the back of the seat. We drove along in silence for so long that I thought she had fallen asleep. The van rumbled pleasantly along.

"Jim," she said.

I glanced at her and then back at the road. "Yes, Anne."

"How did you figure out that my brothers were using Snowy for the squaw?"

I told her. When I'd finished, she said, "They were all surprised that you beat Jeff Davis up."

"I never asked you if you minded," I said.

She sighed thoughtfully. "It didn't occur to me to mind," she said, "because it was their business and your business. You can't have people putting livestock in danger. But then," she added after a pause, "it was my livestock."

"I did it more because it was your livestock," I told her.

There was a pause, and then, "Oh."

"I mean," I added, "if your brothers are putting your llamas in danger, I thought I had better step in."

"They aren't mean people, Jim," she said.

"No?" I asked. I was remembering that night on the town that had ruined my chances with Anne. And they had planned it.

"No," she said gently, "they interfere all the time. More than you know, Jim. But they aren't cruel, only clumsy."

"If you say so."

We fell into silence again, but not uncompanionable. Anne knew that time could change things, and even I supposed—now that I'd gotten the respect of the Hardy boys—that I could get to like them again.

By and by she did fall asleep. My wristwatch showed the time to be past midnight.

We walked the llamas again just before one. This time,

we chose the time and place. Afterward, they settled back down easily. Anne and I switched off driving again at four. I thought I could stay awake a while to talk, but I dozed off almost immediately.

I fell deeply asleep, and it was long afterward that a knocking sound and the smell of smoke slowly brought me around.

"Something must be wrong," Anne said.

"Pull over, Anne!"

She did.

We scrambled out.

"Where are we?" I asked.

"Northern Kentucky."

"Oh, great." I retrieved a flashlight from the van. I pulled up the hood and looked.

"Do you know a lot about cars?" she asked.

"No, and almost nothing about vans, but—well, here's the problem, anyway. This thing—whatever it is—has overheated. I wonder if we dare go a little farther."

"It's the fan," she said. "I think it's gone out. That means trouble if we go too far."

"We've got to get to a phone," I told her.

We both looked around. This was farm country, blue-grass country to be exact.

"We could walk to a farmhouse," Anne suggested. "This is all pasture here."

"I guess we'll have to take the llamas."

"But everyone will be in bed," she added.

"Hey, lights!" I exclaimed. "Blue lights!"

A police car slowed down as it passed and pulled over. We both breathed a sigh of relief.

The state trooper gave us some signals to put up and radioed the dispatcher to send a tow truck.

"The van can't be towed," Anne told him. "We've got livestock in the back."

"Livestock?" he asked. "What kind of livestock?"

Anne opened the back of the van, and we brought out the llamas.

He started at the sight of them and pushed his hat back. "Well, I'll be!" he said. "I'll get a mechanic."

While he was on the radio, Anne said, "What will we do if it costs a lot?"

"Don't worry," I told her. "Anyway, don't worry yet."

"There's one coming," the officer told us. "The dispatcher told him it was likely something in the fan motor."

I imagine there weren't many Kentucky state troopers out at four-thirty in the morning, so when another call came on the radio, he had to take it.

We were left alone.

Anne sighed and leaned against the van, Snow Queen's lead clasped in her hand. "I wonder how long it will take," she said.

I came and stood alongside her.

"I doubt that this mechanic is booked up, whoever he is," I said.

She smiled. "I guess not."

We were quiet again, until at last she said, "My brothers did it to you on purpose, Jim. I guess you knew that. Got you sick and . . . and everything."

"Yes," I said.

"Did you wonder why?" she asked, and without waiting for my answer she said, "They thought you didn't like me. They wanted to make sure I wouldn't feel bad about it."

"Why should they think I didn't like you?" I asked.

"Well, the day that Barn Cat bit you, you were angry. And I thought it was my fault." She switched hands on the lead and looked up at me. "And the night you told me it was all for the best that I didn't finish college, well, I got my feelings hurt."

"I didn't mean to hurt your feelings," I said. "I know now that college meant a lot to you. I thought it was your choice to come back home."

"I was too sensitive," she said. "I made too much out of nothing, and Billy Bob took it to heart. As usual, he had to *do* something."

"I didn't think my opinion was all that important to you," I said.

Anne didn't answer right away. I looked at her, and it seemed as though she were struggling to speak. Her chin trembled.

She swallowed before she could answer. I straightened up and looked more closely at her. The glare from the signals and the emergency lights of the van made the light imperfect, and I leaned closer.

"It was important," she whispered. She looked up at me, and I saw the shine of tears in her eyes.

I leaned even closer, mainly because I could hardly see her and couldn't believe what I was hearing.

"Anne," I said, and my voice sounded more surprised than anything else. Then I found my hand on hers. Her fingers clasped tightly around mine.

"I didn't know it mattered," I said again.

"When you fought Jeff Davis about Snow Queen, then suddenly I thought that maybe you did care."

"I told him myself that I . . ." I caught myself. Maybe this was too soon to say I loved her.

"That you what?" she asked.

"Well, he knows that I care about you," I told her. "Come to think of it, I suppose that the three of them engineered my presence on this trip."

She looked down and then looked up at me. "I helped," she said. "I told them they couldn't come. I was hoping you'd offer." This confession made her lower lip tremble again.

She kept her eyes on mine, and I kissed her.

"But everybody told me you didn't date much," I said. "I thought I'd never have a chance."

"I don't date much. Only the men I want to date," she told

me. "There haven't been many of them."

We kissed again.

"Anne, I think you should know that you're the sweetest, loveliest girl I've ever met," I told her.

"Thank you," she whispered. This time she closed her eyes and reached up with her lips just as I leaned down.

The side of my face made contact against a warm, inquisitive nose. I jerked my head back. Anne gave a little scream and then burst out laughing. Gerda, ears forward, sniffed and nosed her way into the space between us, puzzled as to what Anne and I had been so intent upon. After sniffing us, she leaned forward to inspect the side of the van. Then after a glance at each of us, she strolled back to the end of her lead.

17 - The Mayehuus Farm

The mechanic came and fixed the fan motor on the van. It wasn't a costly job, but the delay was long. By the time we had loaded up again and started the engine, the sun was coming up.

"Four hours to go," I told her. "We won't be too late."

She leaned her head against my shoulder, which I didn't mind at all, and fell asleep.

I felt that my luck must be changing at last. For two hours Anne stayed peacefully asleep, and for the last two hours of the trip we sat side by side and held hands while I drove.

Mr. Mayehuus, jolly as ever, made us welcome at his sprawling farmhouse. We put Gerda in a small pasture alone next to his prize stud, Buckeye, and we and Mr. and Mrs. Mayehuus had an early lunch on their porch.

Their farmhouse had an elegance not found in Horse Creek Valley. It spoke of them as gentle farmers. The breakfast table on the immaculate white porch was wicker, and the chairs were cushioned wicker.

Mrs. Mayehuus served us from a roll-up cart: a complicated chicken salad, rye and pumpernickel, muffins and apple compote, with orange juice and Perrier on the side.

Anne was perfectly at ease with them, and her own

happiness was infectious. We laughed and talked like old friends throughout the meal. And afterwards, as we sipped coffee, I took Anne's hand under the table and held it. Perhaps inspired by us, Mr. and Mrs. Mayehuus sat holding hands as we all talked.

We had a good view of the pasture where Buckeye was grazing. At last Gerda strolled past him to explore her new surroundings, and he got the idea. He would have his chance after Gerda had a week or so on the farm to get adjusted. Some llama breeders take extra care to insure a pregnancy, but Mr. Mayehuus assured us that—given three chances—Buckeye had never missed yet. But Mr. Mayehuus would keep her on his farm three months or so to insure that the breeding was successful before having us drive back to pick her up.

We had to get the van back by Sunday morning, so after a few hours of rest, we climbed into the van again.

Gerda was too interested in her temporary home to notice that we were going, but Snow Queen took a few tentative steps toward the van, as though wanting to go home.

Anne found it hard to leave Snow Queen behind. She didn't shed tears, but she was pensive, and she asked to do the driving, even though she was tired.

But after we were on the road again, I talked about llamas and ranching and the hope of getting a good female from Gerda. Anne cheered up.

The trip back was pleasant and uneventful.

When we pulled into the Hardy farm on Sunday morning, Lem came out to meet us. It was dawn, but he'd gotten up early to wait for us. I suspected that Billy Bob, Bo, and Jefferson Davis were up, too.

I hadn't liked the Hardy brothers, but I realized that in their own clumsy way they really had been trying to make Anne happy. They didn't understand her desire to go to college nor her desire to raise llamas. But they did understand that she'd been interested in me. Love and romance and marriage were things they could understand, and they had wanted those things for Anne.

I opened the van door for her and helped her out. Lem got the message from that simple gesture. He asked me in to breakfast, but I declined.

"I'd like to go get some rest if I can," I told him. I took Anne's hand. "See you at church?"

She smiled. "Sure."

18 - Didee Again

I hesitate, in an age of equality, to say that I rescued Anne or became her protector. It would be an exaggeration in some way, because, after all, her family was not cruel, but rather clumsy.

And yet, I was determined that Anne should do what she wanted without having to answer to her family or be judged by them. She was certainly adult enough, and she had a character that I felt anybody could trust. The time was right to step in and make it clear to her family that I would back Anne in her decisions. I did this by inviting her to come up with me the next Sunday afternoon to visit Didee.

What Lem or the boys had to say about this remained a mystery because Anne never told me. But the next Sunday, after a hurried dinner, the two of us took my car up between the high red banks of the climbing back roads and made our way to Didee's wooden frame house.

It was impossible to telephone ahead to Didee because he had no phone. One was required to drop in and hope that the time was right. But there were appropriate times, and a sleepy Sunday afternoon was one of them.

He met me at the door, obviously glad to see me, and then he saw Anne.

"Why, hello," he said to her, and held out his hand to take hers.

"This is Anne," I told him. "I've told her all about you, and she wanted to come up and meet you herself."

"How do you do?" Anne asked.

"Oh, fine," he told her. He glanced at me. "Is this—," and then he caught himself and said, "is this a sit-down visit? I hope so. The children are gone with Cirrell down to a church dinner."

He had nearly asked me if this was the girl I had told him about. It would have been rather awkward if it hadn't been, and he was wise enough to realize that in time.

We told him that it was a sit-down visit, and he led us inside and brought us cold Pepsis to drink.

"I see my patient is doing fine," I said as the flop-eared dog came waddling out to inspect us. Her toenails clicked on the hardwood floor, and she looked so mournful in the hot weather that I wondered if she hadn't looked better injured.

But when Didee bent to scratch behind her ears, she perked up and sat on the floor against his leg. "Her name's Flopsy," he told us. "She doin' all right now, Vet. Back to her perky ol' self."

My eyes got big, and I refrained from glancing at Anne.

Anne had brought along photos of the llamas, and she showed them to Didee. He examined each with interest at first and then with a more critical eye, as a man will who has purchased livestock and is determining what points to look for.

"Dang nice bunch of animals," he said. "'Cept this kinda hairless one. She the grandma of the herd?"

"She's our mascot," Anne said.

We told him about some of our adventures. I excluded any talk of the squaw, wanting to spare Anne from embarrassment. But we told Didee about the skunk and the trip to Ohio.

He took us out to see the garden, and it was on our walk that he at last told us some of the things I had wondered about.

"Sure, my mama made us biscuits when things was bad—biscuits for breakfast, biscuits for dinner, biscuits for supper," he said, as we strolled past some of the houses. People waved to us now and then. "She had a kind of fat gravy she'd make. Mama didn't have no meas'rin' spoons or cups or nuthin'. Everything was a pinch of this, a big handful, a little handful, and so on. She done it all by sight and by touch. I've seen those chefs on television, y' know, and what with all their gadgets, they can't turn 'em out no better'n Mama did."

"Is your mother still alive?" Anne asked him.

"Oh, no. She died more'n fifteen years ago—tiny scrap of a woman. Wore out, I guess. Aside from raisin' us, she took in washing, y' know. But mercy, she could cook right. Take anything we brought home and make somethin' of it— opposum, coon, fish." He held out his hands to indicate size. "One day, me and my little brother Rodney, we went fishin' with nuthin' but old sticks and lines and some bent pins for hooks, and didn't we land some big ones! Oh my! We run right home to show 'em off, and Mama fried 'em for us, and come the next day one of the neighbor boys told us we'd gone on private property. Fishin' in a white man's pond, where the fish had been stocked. We burned up our poles and lines and prayed we wouldn't go to jail over it." He laughed a rolling, jolly laugh at the memory.

"Your mama took in washing?" Anne asked. "Did she do it with a washboard and tub?"

He glanced at her and nodded. "Sheets and linens, mostly. That was her line. She'd have Pa set the big pot out in the back yard and boil up the bluing for her, and she'd do all the washin' in the morning. Next came the starch— them things that got starched. I'd like to see a man sleep on stiff starched sheets," and he laughed again. "Rodney and me would toss crickets into the starch water to see 'em come out an' stiffen. Mighty cruel, but then we didn't think. Mama'd whip us for it."

He showed Anne the cemetery where some of his relatives were laid, and I realized that it was no accident that Didee had taken me there the first time we'd visited. The cemetery meant something to him—exactly what I wasn't sure. I wondered if it was his touch with a life that—though hard and poor in many ways—had been secure, or if he had simply appointed himself a kind of caretaker over his neighborhood's only monument to soldiers and dead heroes.

"I got a cousin in here," he told Anne. "Wanted to make the army his career. Died in Vietnam. Always volunteered for the hardest places."

For a moment his words were lost on me as I saw in my mind a picture of two young black boys—Didee and Rodney—ornery, free, and happy, for a while unconscious of living in the world that surrounded their piece of Horse Creek Valley. The image in my mind faded in time to hear Anne ask him about his cousin who had died.

By the time our walk had finished, the afternoon was on the wane. We had evening church to attend, and so we said goodbye to him.

The unair-conditioned car was hot from sitting in the sun, but after we had waved to Didee and lost sight of him, Anne slipped her hand into mine and looked at me.

"Did you like him?" I asked her.

"Of course. And I'm glad that Flopsy recovered."

"So am I. She was pretty chewed up when I first saw her."

We drove in silence down the high hills until we were in the valley itself. And for the first time I realized that we were thinking of the same thing—Horse Creek Valley years ago, when Didee had grown up and where Didee had grown up. There was nothing to say because we could only imagine it. At last as we pulled in to the Hardy farm, Anne leaned her head against my shoulder and pushed up a little against my neck. She was thinking—all full of thoughts.

19 - A Happy Ending

I didn't tell Anne that I loved her right away. But it didn't take long. I spent every spare minute with her, sometimes on regular excursions to restaurants in Augusta or Aiken, but most often just walking through the pines together, hand in hand.

Our rainy days we spent poring over books together, looking for new names for the llamas and comparing ideas on stories we had both read.

Anne hated Emerson altogether, and—aside from his Arthurian poems—she disliked Tennyson. Her favorites were Herbert and Donne, and her tastes ran more to the older poets.

I had only a few hours of course work in literature, but Anne was an animated storyteller, and she read aloud well. She taught me to appreciate something of the good and the beautiful and the adventurous that she saw in certain pieces of prose and poetry. All this she did with only a semester of the humanities behind her. Most of her acquaintance with literature came from an excellent high school teacher and her own private readings carried out on scattered Saturday afternoons when she could be spared to go to the library.

"You know, don't you, that I love you, Anne," I said to her one night as we strolled hand in hand among the pines.

She put her other hand into mine and nodded. And she looked at me with a half smile.

"And I want to marry you," I added.

"Yes, Jim," she told me. She clasped my hands tightly.

"Well, what do you think?" I asked.

"I'm ready to marry you. And I don't even remember when I first fell in love with you," she said.

"Anne, I want to promise you that we'll get you through college," I told her. "I promise."

"It would be hard to afford," she said. "In a few years, maybe . . ."

"But Anne, we'll have children in a few years. I'm afraid if we put it off it will never get done."

She hesitated and then said, "All right."

"Jack has offered to sell me a half share of the store," I told her. "The first few years will be tight, but then, the last few years have been tight, too. For me, anyway." And I laughed.

"We could sell the llamas."

"And lose another dream?" I asked. "Will your father let you keep the pasture?"

"Oh my, yes!"

"Let's risk it, then. They only eat grass." I put my arm around her and pulled her close. "I want to make you happy."

She smiled. "I am happy."

"It's too late to have a June wedding," I told her. "How about this fall?"

She nodded. "October, when all the leaves are turning colors."

I was just about to kiss her when we both heard a sighing that might have just been the wind in the pines, but it was followed by a distant human voice, sweet but not articulate.

"What is that?" Anne asked.

"I'm not sure, but I think it's the squaw," I told her. I looked down at her. "Are you afraid? She's never hurt anybody."

"No . . . I . . . but there, it's stopped," she said.

She stayed close to me, which I didn't mind.

Epilogue

The story of how the squaw was impersonated remained a secret to the rest of Horse Creek Valley. Jack never told anybody about it, and the Hardy brothers didn't have much to say on the subject.

I wondered at first how I would get along with the rest of Anne's family. Lem remained as hospitable and friendly as ever, though he must have known of my fight with Jeff Davis. He genuinely wanted Anne to be happy, and I don't think he ever doubted that I wanted to make her happy, too.

Billy Bob, Bo, and Jefferson Davis maintained a cordial attitude toward me. They were never familiar, and as time went by I realized that somehow I had won their respect, whether by winning Anne in the end or by solving the mystery or by beating up Jeff Davis (or by all three), I never knew.

There were plenty of chances to work with the llamas. If becoming a country vet had been impossible, I had at least found—or married into—a field in which I could specialize: llama medicine.

The hopes for the future are still bright. I suppose I'll never be Wagner Nesbitt, but I don't want to be, any more. There are other things to plan for. Anne has taught me the secret of simply being happy. And we take the future one dream at a time.

And what about Barn Cat?

He finally got tired of the band on his paw and chewed the elastic off.